# GORDON'S GAME

# GORDON'S GAME

Six Nations. One Boy. One Big Dream.

## Gordon D'Arcy & Paul Howard

Illustrated by Alan Nolan

PENGUIN

IRELAND

PENGUIN IRELAND

UK | USA | Canada | Ireland | Australia
India | New Zealand | South Africa

Penguin Ireland is part of the Penguin Random House group of companies
whose addresses can be found at global.penguinrandomhouse.com.

Penguin
Random House
UK

First published 2019
001

Text design by 13.25/17.25 pt Garamond MT Std
Typeset by Jouve (UK), Milton Keynes
Printed and bound in Great Britain by Clays Ltd, Elcograf S.p.A.

A CIP catalogue record for this book is available from the British Library

ISBN: 978–1–844–88467–4

www.greenpenguin.co.uk

MIX
Paper from
responsible sources
FSC® C018179

Some people think you need very special qualities to play rugby.

That you have to be as tall as James Ryan . . .

Or as broad as Cian Healy . . .

Or as clever as Conor Murray . . .

Or as skilful as Johnny Sexton . . .

Or as brave as Bundee Aki.

Do you know what I found out?

You don't need to be any of those things.

It doesn't matter how big you are.

Or how strong you are.

Or even how old you are.

Because on the field, there is a job for everyone.

That's why I fell in love with the game – because every player has something different that he or she can contribute.

And it's all those contributions added together that make a team.

So don't let anyone tell you that you're too short, or too skinny, or too slow, or too young to be a rugby player.

All you really need is the passion to work hard at your game – and the good sense not to let success go to your head.

I learned that the hard way.

Every player has his or her own story to tell. This is mine.

And every single word of it is cross-my-heart-and-hope-to-die true. I know that because it happened to me – even the bit about the angry chicken!

# 1 'What is THIS?'

I can still remember the day I discovered rugby.

It was a Saturday afternoon and I heard Dad shouting in the living room. I wondered had I done something wrong – again? I stuck my head around the door.

'Is this about the broken bathroom window?' I asked.

He didn't seem to hear me. He was sitting in front of the TV, watching what *seemed* to be a movie. There was a lot of shouting and screaming and there were bodies lying everywhere, some wearing bandages and all of them covered in mud.

'COME ON, IRELAND!' he shouted. 'DO SOMETHING!'

Dad was so transfixed by what was happening on the screen that he didn't even notice me sit down on the sofa next to him. Very quickly, I was transfixed, too. It turned out that it wasn't a war movie after all – because suddenly a strangely shaped ball flashed across the screen and they all went haring after it.

'What is *this*?' I asked.

He turned his head, seeing me for the first time.

'This,' he said, 'is RUGBY!'

I'd only ever *heard* about rugby before. My older brother, Ian, played it, but I used to laugh at him as he set off for training, already wearing his boots and his gumshield, with a bandage wrapped around his head to make sure that his ears stayed on – or at least that's what he told me!

So *this* is what he'd been playing all that time?

I watched in silent awe. Players were smashing into other players and sending each other flying. They were tackling each other around the waist and throwing each other to the ground. They were allowed to do things that I could only dream of doing when I played hurling.

'Who's playing?' I asked, watching the white and green players trying to get past each other, like a big, mad game of Red Rover.

'It's Ireland against England,' Dad said.

It was without a doubt the most exciting thing I had EVER seen on TV!

'Wait a minute,' Dad said suddenly. 'What was that about a broken window?'

'Er, nothing,' I said.

'Were you trying to chip golf balls through that open bathroom window again?' he asked.

Mum always said we were the local glazier's best customer. And that was down to me! As he replaced yet another pane of glass, Dad would shake his head and say, 'That fella's children are going to be very well educated. I should know – I'm the one who's putting them through college!'

'Gordon,' he said now, 'please don't tell me I've to replace another window?'

'Let's talk about that later,' I said. 'We don't want to miss anything in the match, do we?'

Dad suddenly jumped to his feet. 'THAT'S IT, CLOHESSY!' he yelled. 'GO ON, BRADLEY! DANAHER'S THERE! THAT'S IT! NOW, WALLACE, GIVE IT TO GEOGHEGAN! GIVE IT TO GEOGHEGAN! *GIVE IT TO GEOGHEGAN!*'

He gave it to Geoghegan.

Now, Geoghegan had two players in white standing between him and the line. But it was like he flicked a switch and found a gear that no one else had. He burned past the two England players and

slammed the ball down, one-handed, right on the line. Dad roared. I didn't know exactly what had happened, but *I* jumped to my feet and roared, too.

'THAT WAS A TRY!' Dad said. 'SIMON GEOGHEGAN, YOU BEAUTY! WE'RE BEATING ENGLAND AT TWICKENHAM, GORDON! IRELAND ARE BEATING

ENGLAND AT TWICKENHAM!' Before I knew it, he had lifted me up into the air.

In the end, Ireland won! It was 13–12. It was a really historic day. One of the biggest in Irish sport, according to Dad. The Ireland players looked absolutely exhausted when the ref blew the whistle, but they were smiling and holding their hands up and the crowd went absolutely crazy.

And from that moment on, rugby was the only game for me!

The next morning, I went out to the shed in the back garden. After twenty minutes of poking around broken umbrellas and smelly tins of paint, I found one of Ian's old rugby balls. I took it outside. I stood there, turning it over in my hands. I'd never liked playing with it before because I couldn't understand why it wasn't round, like most balls. I didn't know if you were supposed to kick it at one of the pointed ends or kick it in the middle. First, I tried kicking one of the pointed ends – and it really hurt my foot. It was like kicking concrete! So I tried it again. This time, I held the ball sideways, a pointed end in either hand, and I kicked it as hard as I could. The ball travelled about ten feet into the air, then came down, hit the ground and bounced unexpectedly to the right, sending the cat running for cover. Ian used to say, 'The shape of the ball is one of the things that makes rugby so exciting, Gordon! You can never take for granted what's going to happen next!'

I apologized to the cat, then had another go. Then another. And another. I practised all morning, all afternoon and all evening. I tried kicking different parts of the ball, using different parts of my foot. After hours and hours of practice, I discovered that the best way to kick the ball out of my hands was to hold it upright, with one end pointing up at the sky and the other end pointing down at the ground, then tilt the top end slightly towards me, before making contact with the ball three-quarters of the way down, using the laces of my shoes. By the time I learned this, I had broken the window of the shed, knocked several slates off the roof of the house, destroyed a washing line full of clothes and traumatized the poor cat. But once I got the hang of it, I could get the ball to go exactly where I wanted it to go – and even bounce the way I wanted it to bounce.

After that day, the rugby ball was hardly ever out of my hands.

I'd run round the garden with it, imagining that I was evading tacklers every step of the way, with a feint one way, then a flick of my hips and a change of direction to leave the great English centre Will Carling in my dust.

I'd imagine I could hear the commentator George Hamilton's voice: 'HE'S GOT D'ARCY OUTSIDE HIM! HERE GOES GORDON D'ARCY! AND D'ARCY GOES FOR THE CORNER! AND D'ARCY IS IN! AND IRELAND ARE IN FRONT!'

I sometimes stopped and looked at my reflection in the window of the car, running my fingers through my hair to try to get it to stand up the way Simon Geoghegan's hair stood up.

And when I sat down for meals, I had the ball resting on my lap underneath the table. I even took it to bed with me, falling asleep with it clutched to my chest.

Then, one Saturday morning, Dad stepped out into the garden and walked over to me.

'Open your mouth,' he said.

I did what he told me and he shoved a gumshield into it. Then he produced a roll of sticky bandaging and he wrapped my head with it, spinning me around and around as he did so.

'What are you doing?' I asked.

Except, with the gumshield in my mouth, it sounded more like: '*Hot harr hoo hooing?*'

'I'm taking you to rugby,' he said.

'*Hug hee?*'

I took the gumshield out and tried it again.

'Rugby?' I asked.

'That's right,' Dad said. 'You can't play by your-self forever – even if George Hamilton *is* singing your praises!'

Oops. I thought I was doing that voice *inside* my head! He handed me a pair of Ian's old boots.

'They're WAY too big for me,' I said.

'You can wear two pairs of socks,' he said. 'There's a pair inside them there. Now, into the car with you. We don't want to be late.'

I put the second pair of socks on over my own socks, then pulled on the boots, which were still a bit loose, but I could walk in them.

'You'll grow into them,' Dad said. 'Now, come on.'

We drove to Park Lane and he parked the car in front of a field. There were twenty or thirty other boys standing around, waiting for training to start.

'What's this team called?' I asked.

He said, 'They're called Wexford Wanderers!'

Wexford was the town where we lived. It was a beautiful town, right near the sea, in the south-eastern corner of Ireland. Picture the map of Ireland. Then picture it as a teddy bear. Wexford is a pimple on its bum.

Or maybe not a pimple. Let's just call it a beauty spot.

A beauty spot on Ireland's bum.

'Wexford Wanderers are the business,' Dad said. 'They taught your brother how to play the game.'

We walked across the field towards the other kids. In the middle of them stood a very tall man with a big pot belly and stick-thin legs. He had a friendly face and was wearing a woolly hat, as well as shorts, which showed off his knobbly knees.

'My name is Jimmy O'Connor,' he said, spinning the ball in his hands. 'And today you're going to learn all about rugby. I'm not sure if there's a future Simon Geoghegan among you lot. But there's only one way for me to find out how good you all are. And that's by doing this!'

He kicked the ball high in the air. He kicked it harder than I'd ever seen a ball kicked before.

We all looked up, watching it disappear into the sky, until we had to strain our eyes just to see it. And then it started to fall to Earth again.

'Forget what's going on around you,' Jimmy said, 'and just focus on the ball!'

Seconds later, it hit the ground with a thud, then it shot back towards me like a bullet from a gun, hitting me full in the stomach. I managed to hold it, but I was winded for a second.

'Well?' Jimmy shouted. 'What are you all waiting for? Play rugby!'

Suddenly, all of the other boys were running towards me like a herd of stampeding animals. Ferocious ones, with their gumshields bared.

I gulped.

Then I tucked the ball under my arm and took off in the opposite direction.

I zigzagged my way around the field . . . evading every pair of grabbing hands . . . then, when someone did catch me, I squirmed until I managed to get loose . . . and the chase resumed.

It was exhaustion that got me in the end. My legs just gave way and very quickly I disappeared under a mountain of bodies . . .

But I still had the ball! I never let go of the ball!

A moment later, Jimmy arrived on the scene.

'Are you okay in there?' he said. It was like he was talking to someone who'd been buried in a landslide. 'Give me a sign that you're still alive.'

From the bottom of that pile of human rubble, I managed to push the ball out and ground it with my two hands.

Jimmy laughed. 'I think we'll call that a try,' he said. 'What's your name in there?'

'*Horhon*,' I said. '*Horhon Harhy.*'

'Horhon Harhy? What kind of a name is that?'

I spat out my gumshield.

'Gordon,' I said, trying to catch my breath. 'My name is Gordon D'Arcy.'

'Well, Gordon D'Arcy,' he replied, 'something tells me this won't be the last time I hear that name.'

# 2  Do NOT Try This at Home!

'GORDON D'ARCY! What in the name of all that's holy have you done NOW?'

It was Mum's voice, and she sounded angry.

To be honest, I was kind of used to hearing those words. I was in trouble pretty often. You could even say it was the story of my life.

I wasn't a bad kid. Everyone agreed on that point. I just had what Dad liked to call AN EXCESS OF ENTHUSIASM. I was always trying to be helpful. And that's when the trouble usually started.

There was the time, for instance, when I heard Mum complain about how quickly my little sister Megan was growing. 'She doesn't fit into *any* of her old clothes anymore!' she told Dad.

Well, I came up with what I thought was a great solution to that problem. That night, while the rest of the family were tucked up in bed, I crept into Megan's room and gathered up all of her clothes. I brought them downstairs and outside to the greenhouse. I took a bucket and I filled it with Magic-Grow, a foul-smelling, yellowy-greeny liquid that Dad used to help him grow the BIGGEST tomatoes in all of Wexford.

I dipped every item of clothing that Megan owned into the bucket of Magic-Grow, then I hung everything on the washing line to dry.

I thought it would be a surprise for Mum when she woke up the following morning. It was a surprise alright – but not in a good way. Because Megan's clothes didn't actually grow. As a matter of fact, they SHRANK! And not only did they shrink, the Magic-Grow turned everything a colour that could best be described as, well . . . snot green.

I had to lie low for a few hours after that lot was discovered hanging from the washing line!

Another time, Dad mentioned how much he hated the colour of the family car. It was white – which meant that it got very, very dirty and Dad had to wash it at least once a week.

'The next time I buy a car,' he said one day, as he sprayed it with the hose, 'it's going to be black!'

And I thought, Why should he have to wait? The

man worked hard! He deserved to drive the car of his dreams now!

So that evening, while Mum and Dad were watching TV, I went outside to the shed and found a large tin of black paint. I opened the lid, stuck a brush in it and gave our boring white car a very nice makeover.

Unfortunately, what was in the tin wasn't paint at all, but creosote, a kind of thick, black tar usually used for painting fences.

The car ended up the colour Dad wanted alright, but it was destroyed. The creosote hardened. And when Dad tried to scrape it off, it took all the white paint off with it. Let's just say, he ended up buying a new car a lot sooner than he'd expected.

And now it seemed I'd messed up again somehow, because I was hearing those very familiar words:

'GORDON D'ARCY! What in the name of all that's holy have you done NOW?'

All I had done was arrange a surprise picnic for my family to celebrate the first day of the school summer holidays. For ages, Mum and Dad had been talking about packing up the car and bringing us off somewhere for a family picnic – me, Megan, Ian and my older sister, Shona. They had it all planned, but the night before we were supposed to go, Dad got a phone call to say that he had to work.

Dad was a bank manager, so he spent his days sitting outside a vault, minding all of the money for Wexford, which he told me ran into the GAZILLIONS.

He was a very important man, which meant he couldn't say no when he was told that he was needed for the entire weekend. So, much to our disappointment, the picnic was cancelled.

Lying in bed that night, I had an idea – and it was one of my better ones. What if *I* arranged a picnic for us – in the back garden? If I got up nice and early, then got straight to work, I could have the whole thing ready in time for breakfast. We could all enjoy an early morning feast together as a family before waving Dad off to work.

What could go wrong? I was absolutely certain that this was one of the best ideas I'd ever had. It was foolproof!

So, early the next morning, while everyone in the house was still sound asleep, I crept downstairs to the kitchen. Slowly, and as quietly as I could, I removed every single item of food from the cupboard, the fridge and the freezer, then laid them out on the kitchen table. There was:

One raw chicken.

One block of cheese.

One jar of honey.

One bottle of milk.

Four pots of strawberry yoghurt.

Half a packet of ham slices.

Half a jar of blackcurrant jam.

One cucumber.

One packet of mince.

Three Hobnobs – stale.

One bag of frozen peas.

Two eggs.

Six tomatoes.

One jar of mustard.

One onion.

One packet of frozen fish.

One box of Corn Flakes.

One bottle of red lemonade.

One bag of frozen sweetcorn.

A loaf of bread.

Half a carton of orange juice.

One punnet of Wexford strawberries.

One block of vanilla ice cream.

Six pork chops.

One box of Rice Krispies.

Some broccoli.

Some baked beans in a cup.

Half a pound of butter.

And one bag of frozen chips.

It was loads! I was sure I could put on a spread fit for a king or queen with this lot.

I took Mum's good Christmas tablecloth from the drawer, brought it outside to the garden and spread it out on the grass. Then I took some plates and some cutlery and I set a place on the tablecloth for everyone in the family. One for Mum. One for Dad. One for Ian. One for Shona. One for little Megan. And one for me.

Next, I carried all of the contents of the cupboard,

fridge and freezer outside and laid them out on the tablecloth. It took quite a while, but I was mightily impressed with the result. I had to admit, I was proving to be quite the entertainer.

But then I thought to myself, Wait a minute, Gordon – where's the cake? You can't have a surprise party without a cake!

So I decided to bake one. Yes, the good ideas just kept on coming!

The only problem was that I had no idea how to actually *make* a cake. I took out a mixing bowl and tried to remember all of the ingredients that I'd seen Mum put into hers.

There was definitely flour. I was pretty much sure of that. Yes, cakes one hundred percent DEFINITELY had flour in them.

And sugar. You couldn't have a cake without sugar. But what else?

Salt? It sounded wrong but at the same time it sounded right. Okay, just a *little* bit of salt, then.

Breadcrumbs? Yes, that's obviously what gives a cake its bready texture.

What about some coffee granules? Everybody loves coffee cake, don't they? So I tipped the entire jar of instant coffee into the bowl.

Butter. Oh no, I'd already put the butter outside

in the garden. So I used olive oil instead – the entire bottle.

And then, just to give it an extra twist, I threw in some random ingredients:

Two fistfuls of parsley.
Three fistfuls of Coco Pops.
A mug of chilli powder.
Two teaspoons of marmalade.
A splash of vinegar.
Some toothpaste – spearmint.
A sprinkle of cloves.
Three beetroots – thinly chopped.
Six tablespoons of custard powder.
And, why not, another splash of vinegar!

I mixed it all up in the bowl, then I put the bowl in the oven and turned the temperature up to high.

I went back outside to make sure everything was just so. A fox was helping himself to the pork chops and I had to shoo him away. I tidied the place-settings again, then I smiled, pleased with my work.

I checked the time. It was almost 7.00 a.m. It was still a little bit early to wake the rest of the house, so I decided to have a little power nap on the sofa.

It was the smoke alarm that woke Mum. And it was Mum's screams from the kitchen that woke me.

'GORDON D'ARCY! What in the name of all that's holy have you done NOW?'

I opened my eyes.

Uh-oh.

'WHY IS THE KITCHEN FULL OF SMOKE?' she yelled. 'AND WHY IS EVERY PIECE OF FOOD WE OWN SITTING IN THE BACK GARDEN?'

It was later that night, after Dad had returned home from work, that I heard him and Mum discussing what I'd done. My bedroom was directly above the kitchen, and if I put my ear to the floor and covered the other ear with my hand, I could hear everything that was being said below.

'How about some cake?' Mum asked. 'It's burnt to a cinder but it's got toothpaste and beetroot in it. And I think I can smell cloves!'

Dad sighed. 'What are we going to do with him?' he asked.

'I've no idea,' Mum replied. 'I mean, he's a good boy.'

'He's a *very* good boy,' Dad said. 'He just has all this . . . energy.'

'And enthusiasm,' Mum added.

'Oh, WAY too much enthusiasm,' Dad said. 'He's just so eager to please. Sometimes, I think he's like a golden Labrador with a big, red bow around his neck!'

They both laughed. I'd hoped they'd see the funny side of it eventually.

'Maybe he could go to my sister's,' Mum suggested. 'For a little holiday, I mean. He could have fun with his cousins there.'

'Could be the making of him,' Dad said.

What? Was I hearing them right? Were they really considering sending me away? And how long would I be gone for? A week? A month? Or would it be . . .

I gulped.

. . . forever?

I ran downstairs and pushed open the door of the kitchen. Mum and Dad took one look at me – rugby ball stuck in the crook of my arm – and they smiled at me.

'Gordon,' Dad said, 'how would you like to spend a week or two on the family farm?'

It was news to me that there *was* a family farm.

'I didn't know we had a farm?' I said.

'It's your Auntie Kathleen and your Uncle Tim's farm,' Mum said. 'It might be a good place for you to, you know, get rid of some of that energy of yours!'

'A farm?' I said. I was suddenly very excited. 'I'd love that.'

Mum put a slice of cake in front of me.

'Here,' she said, grinning at me. 'You must share your recipe with me. Unless you're planning to sell it to Mr Kipling, of course.'

I took one look at it. It looked absolutely revolting. And it smelled even worse. I may have overdone it with the vinegar.

'I'm, er, not really hungry,' I said. 'I think I'll just go upstairs to pack.'

## 3  *Down on the Farm*

It was my first day waking up on the farm. I was in a deep, deep sleep, enjoying a really exciting dream in which I scored a last-minute try against England to help Ireland win the Six Nations Championship. Then, just as I was being lifted up on my teammates' shoulders, I found myself being shaken awake.

'Gordon!' a voice said. 'Time to get up, Gordon. Come on, let's go!'

It was Uncle Tim. He was a cheerful man, who always wore a flat cap even when he was indoors. And his trousers were always pulled high above his waist, with a length of baling twine serving as a belt.

'What time is it?' I asked.

I was still clutching my rugby ball under the duvet.

'Four o'clock,' he answered.

'Four o'clock?' I said. 'Are you telling me I've been asleep all day?'

'No,' he said, seeming to find this funny for some reason, 'it's four o'clock in the *morning*!'

I had no idea there *was* a four o'clock in the morning. And, I had to admit, I much preferred the afternoon one.

'Why are you waking me in the middle of the night?' I asked.

'Because the middle of the night is when a farmer's day begins,' said Uncle Tim, switching on the light. 'I'll see you in the kitchen.'

'What?' I said, my eyes blinking to adjust to the brightness. 'You mean NOW?'

'No.' Uncle Tim replied. 'Any time in the next thirty seconds would be grand!'

Slowly and wearily, I pulled on my clothes, then I trudged downstairs to the kitchen, my eyelids feeling like they weighed a tonne each.

My cousins – Anne, Clare, Mary, Teresa and Helena – were already sitting around the table. Aunt Kathleen was piling slices of buttered toast onto a plate and they were disappearing just as quickly.

'The thing is,' I said, 'I was led to believe that this was going to be a holiday.'

Auntie Kathleen laughed. 'It *is* a holiday,' she said. 'That's why we let you have a lie-in until four!'

I sat down – the ball on my lap – and I bit into a slice of toast. Being awake this early was not natural. I said it as well:

'This is not natural!'

'Let me see them hands,' said Uncle Tim.

I held out my hands and he examined them.

'They're soft!' he said. 'They're the hands of a boy who's never done an honest day's work in his life!'

'I'm only a kid,' I reminded him.

'Well, a kid or not,' he said, 'today, you're going to learn all about farming. It's the best job in the world. We work hard and we get rewards from what we put in. Now, put that rugby ball down and follow me. You, too, girls.'

I had a BAD feeling about this.

He led us all into a barn. The smell inside was so bad it would be impossible to describe in words – except to ask you to think of the smelliest thing you've ever smelled in your life.

Done it?

Well, this was TEN TIMES WORSE than even THAT!

The smell turned out to be quite literally . . . poo.

Chicken poo!

A *lot* of chicken poo. Because this was a barn where dozens and dozens of chickens lived. It was where they laid their eggs. And when they weren't laying eggs, they were either eating or they were pooing. That's all they did. Laid eggs, ate and pooed. From one end of the day to the other.

'Now,' said Uncle Tim, 'we're here to collect the delicious eggs these chickens have laid this morning.'

He pointed to a narrow slit at the bottom of each of the coops.

'What you have to do,' he said, 'is to put your hand through the gap there, find the egg and pull it out.'

That doesn't sound too difficult, I thought.

So I slipped my hand through one of the gaps and I blindly patted the floor of the coop in search of an egg. Suddenly, I felt a sharp pain on the back of my hand.

'Ouch!' I said, pulling it out. 'The chicken in there just pecked me!'

The girls all laughed.

'That's Princess Layer,' Uncle Tim said. 'And of course she pecked you! You were trying to steal her eggs!'

'That's because you told me to!' I argued back.

'Yes,' he said, 'but you have to be quick about it!'

Through a gap in the wooden slats, Princess Layer gave me a hard, steely-eyed stare, like she was daring me to try it again.

'Quick?' I said. 'Oh, I can be quick. Quick is my middle –'

I pushed my hand in again. And then . . .

'AAARRRGGGHHH!!!'

Princess Layer pecked me again. Except this time it was harder *and* sorer!

My cousins thought it was hilarious.

'I don't think she's too fond of you,' laughed Helena.

'Teresa,' Uncle Tim said, 'show your cousin how it's done.'

Teresa stepped forward. In a blur of movement, she slipped her hand through the gap, then, a split-second later, pulled it out again, clutching an egg between her tiny fingers.

'Just copy the girls,' Uncle Tim said. 'I'll be back in two hours, then it's on to the next job.'

Off he went.

I wasn't going to copy the girls. And I wasn't going to risk life and limb just to collect a few measly eggs either.

'Where are you going?' Helena asked.

'I'm taking measures to protect myself,' I answered.

I went back into the house. In a drawer in the kitchen I found a pair of oven gloves . . .

They were essential for a job like this.

Then I took two cushions from the sofa in the living room. Using a roll of masking tape, I fixed one on my front, covering my stomach and chest, then one to my back, wrapping the tape around and around my body.

Next, I found a colander in the kitchen that my Aunt Kathleen used for draining the water off the vegetables. I put it on my head, then I pulled on the oven gloves and returned to the chicken barn.

When my cousins saw me in my homemade suit of armour, they fell about laughing.

'Oh, Gordon,' Anne said, 'you're way too soft to ever be a farmer!'

But I had the last laugh because I didn't get pecked once! I didn't get many eggs either – and I managed to drop or crush most of the ones I did get in those big, awkward oven gloves. But the chickens couldn't hurt me, and that was all that mattered.

When Uncle Tim returned, he led us all outside to explain to us our second chore of the day:

Milking the cows!

'I don't think you're going to need your suit of armour for this job!' Clare said.

I wasn't going to take any chances, though. I decided to leave it on for now.

Milking a cow turned out to be not quite as dangerous as stealing eggs from an angry chicken. But it was DISGUSTING!

First, you had to wash the cow's teats using soapy

water, then dry them off. Next, you had to rub this jelly-like stuff into your hands. Then you had to put an empty bucket under the cow's udders. And finally, squatting down, you had to wrap your hand around each teat in turn and pull downwards to release the milk into the bucket.

As it turned out, I was glad I didn't remove my suit of armour because Melanie, the cow I was told to milk, kept trying to bite me. Luckily, I had the colander and the cushions to protect me.

'You need to get closer to her,' Anne suggested, 'so she can't reach you with her teeth.'

'I can't get any closer to her,' I told her, 'because the milk keeps splashing out of the bucket into my face!'

Like I said – disgusting!

When the milking was done, the insides of my legs ached from squatting down for so long. I had filled one bucket, but my cousins had filled six buckets each. I thought it might be time to go for a nap, but then we were given our third job of the morning:

Stopping the crows from eating the corn!

Uncle Tim and Auntie Kathleen had scarecrows all over their fields. They were basically wooden crosses, hammered into the ground, then dressed in clothes and stuffed with straw to make them look like humans. But crows are very smart birds and it doesn't take them long to figure out that they're not real.

That was why it was necessary to have real-life scarecrows chasing them away from the crops.

In other words . . .

US!

But, as well as being smart, crows are very, VERY persistent. We chased them away from one part of the field, then we turned around only to discover that they were munching away on the corn at the other end of the field.

So back and forth we had to run all morning, waving our arms and shouting, 'GO AWAY, GREEDY CROWS!'

It was exhausting – especially for me, because I was still wearing my protective suit.

After lunch, we were given our next job:

Digging potatoes!

This seemed like easy work at first, especially compared to chasing crows. You took your shovel, pressed it into the ground with your foot and turned over the soil, then bent down to pick the potatoes out of it. After a while, though, it really started to hurt my back.

But at least the potatoes didn't peck my hands. And by the middle of the afternoon, I had grown confident enough to finally remove my suit of armour. It was a relief because I was seriously sweating in it.

Uncle Tim went away and returned a couple of hours later to give us our next job of the day:

Baling hay!

Uncle Tim drove the combine-harvester – a huge, mechanical monster that ate up entire fields of dried grass, then spat out hay, which would eventually be used as bedding for the cows. Then he used another piece of machinery to compress the hay into bales, which were large and shaped like a cube. It was our job to stack the bales, ready for the tractor, which would come along with its big vice grip and carry about ten of them off together.

I decided I should have some fun while I worked. I stacked the bales in such a way that I created a fort out of them . . .

And I pretended that it was under attack from an enemy army . . .

I suddenly realized that my fort gave me a place to hide so I wouldn't be given any more jobs. I crawled inside and stayed quiet. I'd worked so hard that day, I managed to fall asleep inside.

I had no idea how long I'd been asleep, but I was awoken by the sound of a tractor engine that seemed uncomfortably close to where I was lying. Suddenly, the walls of the fort began to close in on me. The tractor was picking up the bales of hay that made up my fort!

I really was under attack!

I now had a wall of hay in my face and I felt myself being lifted into the air. My cousins laughed themselves silly when they saw Uncle Tim lifting the bales with the tractor and my little legs sticking out of the bottom!

As the day neared its end, my cousins went into the house to help Auntie Kathleen prepare the dinner. But Uncle Tim had one last job for me to do before I was finished – and, he said, it was the most difficult job of all.

'What could be more difficult than collecting eggs, milking cows, chasing crows, picking potatoes and baling hay?' I said.

'Catching the chickens,' he answered with a smile.

He took me to a large yard with a dirt floor just behind the chicken barn. There were about sixty chickens there, stalking around the place, pecking the ground.

'Why do *I* have to catch them?' I said. 'Who let them out?'

'They have to be let out for exercise and for food,' Uncle Tim explained. 'Then, at night, they have to go back indoors again, so they don't get eaten by foxes. But you have to catch them one by one and carry them all inside.'

I just shrugged my shoulders. I mean, how hard could it be – right?

'The problem is,' Uncle Tim said, 'chickens do NOT like going to bed. They're worse than kids that way. So if it's too much for you, don't be afraid to ask the girls for help.'

Ask the girls for help? I didn't need anyone's help to put away a few chickens.

'I'll be grand,' I assured Uncle Tim.

There was one chicken standing just in front of me. I bent down to pick her up. I put my two hands around her body and lifted her up off the ground.

'See?' I said. 'Easy!'

But then she started flapping her wings wildly, while trying to peck and scratch at me. I had no choice but to let her go and she flew across to the other side of the yard.

Uncle Tim laughed. He said, 'Go easy on him, Princess Layer, there's a good girl!'

It was *her*! I should have known.

'And remember,' Uncle Tim told me, 'don't be too proud to ask for help!'

Then off he went.

I wouldn't be asking anyone for help. No, this was a battle I was determined to win by myself.

I eyed Princess Layer across the yard and Princess Layer stared straight back at me. She seemed to be saying, 'Bring it on, Gordon! Let me see what you've got!'

I walked forward slowly in a sort of crouch, zig-zagging towards her to try to corner her. I got closer and closer to her. She didn't move a muscle until I was right in front of her and reaching down to take her into my hands.

And then suddenly . . .

FLAP! FLAP! FLAP! FLAP! FLAP!

She reared up at me, making her body huge, and started beating her two wings to warn me off. I have to admit, I straightened up and took a step back-wards, then she flew straight at me, making this horrible noise:

'BWWWOOOWWWKKK!!! BWWWOOO-WWWKKK!!!'

I was forced to drop to the ground as she flew straight at my face, then past me.

I wasn't going to be beaten. I turned around and ran after her. But she was fast and she was slippery.

I chased her this way . . .

And I chased her that way . . .

And every time I thought I'd caught her . . .

She flapped her wings and made that awful noise again:

'BWWWOOOWWWKKK!!! BWWWOOO-WWWKKK!!!'

And she scratched at me . . .

And pecked at me . . .

And managed to wriggle free again.

This went on for what seemed like an hour. There were sixty chickens and I hadn't managed to put ONE to bed yet!

I sat on the ground with my back against the wall of the chicken shed. I shook my head, while Princess Layer strutted around the yard, full of herself. She went:

'BWOCK, BWOCK, BWOCK – BWOOOC-CCKKK!'

Which sounded like laughter to me. It sounded like mocking laughter.

I'd had enough.

I stood up and went into the house. My cousins were helping Auntie Kathleen and Uncle Tim was sitting in his armchair next to the fire, reading his newspaper.

'Well?' he said. 'Are they all away?'

'No,' I told him.

'No?' he asked. 'What have you been doing for the last hour?'

'I gave up! It's too hard!'

'You gave up? But didn't I tell you to ask the girls if you needed help?'

'It's impossible!'

'It's not impossible,' he said. 'We do it every night.'

'Princess Layer has a vendetta against me,' I told him.

They all thought that was HILARIOUS, of course.

'I'll go,' said Anne.

'I'll give you a hand,' said Clare.

Then Mary, Teresa and Helena followed them out the door, too.

'How do you people LIVE like this?' I asked.

Uncle Tim put down his newspaper and looked at me.

'Gordon,' he said, 'life isn't always easy. Sure, there's a lot of pleasure to be got from it, but to enjoy the pleasure you have to accept a certain amount of pain. Do you understand me?'

'No,' I told him. 'I have literally no idea what you're talking about.'

Auntie Kathleen laughed.

'What Tim is trying to tell you,' she said, 'is that you get out of life what you put into it. If you work hard, then you'll get your rewards. And you'll enjoy them more because you worked for them.'

The girls arrived back into the kitchen.

'All done,' Helena said.

*What?* They'd been gone less than five minutes.

'Teamwork makes the dream work,' said Clare, then she took out the dinner plates, while Anne polished the glasses and Mary, Teresa and Helena set the table.

Auntie Kathleen opened the oven door and took out a tray of roast potatoes. I suddenly realized just how hungry I was. The smell of those potatoes made me drool like a dog.

'How's your back?' Uncle Tim asked me.

'My what?' I asked.

'Your back,' he said. 'You were complaining earlier that it was sore – from bending down to pick the potatoes.'

'Oh, yeah,' I said. 'It's still a bit stiff alright.'

'Well, what you're smelling right now are the potatoes you picked today. And because you picked them yourself, they're going to taste like the nicest potatoes you've ever eaten in your life.'

They were trying to teach me a valuable lesson. But the thing about valuable lessons is that you don't always understand them at the time.

In my case, it would take a long time for the penny to finally drop.

# 4  I'm a Wanderer

I survived the farm and Mum and Dad thought I
was a little less wild when I got home. But that was
because I was playing rugby morning, noon and
night, so there wasn't much time to get into trouble.
As I got bigger and learned more about the game,
the best thing in my whole life, the thing I loved to
do most was play for the great Wexford Wanderers, with Jimmy O'Connor as my coach. We were
the best junior rugby team in the whole of County
Wexford.

Although that was open to debate. We'll come
back to that later.

I was the team's hooker – right in the centre of the
front row. I chose to play there because it was the
position of Keith Wood, who had replaced Simon
Geoghegan as my favourite player in the entire world.

Keith Wood played for Ireland and Munster. Some people called him The Raging Potato because, well, from a certain angle he did actually look like a very angry potato.

But he played rugby like a very angry tornado.

Jimmy always said that the hookers were the most important players on the field, even though most of the work they did went unnoticed.

'Your kickers, your wingers and your full-backs, they're the fellas that get all the attention,' he said. 'But without a good hooker, they'd never get the ball in their hands in the first place.'

It was the hooker's job to throw the ball into the lineout. That was all I really knew at first. But before I played in the position for the first time, Jimmy sat me down and explained my responsibilities to me.

'When the ball is fed into the scrum,' he said, 'it's *your* job to try to win it by hooking it with your feet and passing it back, so that it eventually pops out to Peter.'

Peter was Peter Rackard, our scrum-half and my best friend on the team. Peter was small for his age and wore glasses with lenses that were as thick as the bulletproof glass in the bank where my dad worked. Obviously, he took them off to play rugby, which meant he was pretty much blind – although I don't *ever* remember him making a bad pass. He always seemed to know where to throw the ball as if by instinct.

As a hooker, I was expected to carry the ball in open play and win territory for the team. But I was also kind of skilful, so I was also expected to score tries – which, I'm happy to say, I often did.

By the time I was coming to the end of my years with Wexford Wanderers, I'd developed a bit of a reputation for myself as a player.

Let's just say I was being talked about in Wexford.

One day, in the car park of the club, I overheard

Jimmy telling my dad that I was good. And he said it in such a serious voice that I knew he really meant it.

'How good?' Dad asked him. 'Do you mean as good as his brother was at his age?'

'Better,' Jimmy said. 'He has the potential to be one of the greats, Mr D'Arcy.'

In a few months, I would be going away to boarding school – to Clongowes Wood College, in far-away County Kildare. Ian had gone there before me and had been the star of the school team. The other students even had a song about him, which they sang whenever he played. It was called 'Mill 'Em, Darce' and it went like this:

> *Mill 'em, Darce!*
> *Na na na!*
> *Mill 'em, Darce!*
> *Na na na!*
> *You better hope and pray*
> *You don't get in his way,*
> *Mill 'em, Darce!*
> *Na na na!*

Whenever he came home for the weekend, Ian would tell me all about his exploits on the rugby field. He'd fill me in on the battles and the rivalries.

And he'd quote words of advice and pieces of wisdom he'd heard from Vinnie Murray, the famous Clongowes coach, who Ian said was a legend in the schools game.

I would listen to these stories absolutely spellbound. Then we would go out onto the landing, beside the stairs, and I would stand very, very still so he could practise his tackling on me.

BAM!!!

We really did test the strength of the banister.

Clearly, being a human tackle bag for Ian didn't do me any harm because now I was making my own mark on the game with the Wanderers. Being knocked over by Ian again and again had toughened me up no end, which was exactly what a hooker needs.

The day arrived when I was to play my very last game for Wexford Wanderers. And it was a big one. We were in the final of the Wexford Cup – against our bitterest rivals.

We were sure we were the best team in Wexford, even in the country! But there was only one serious opponent that could steal that title from us . . .

# THE GOREY GLADIATORS!

You could say they were our arch-enemies, because we disliked them every bit as much as they disliked us. Whenever we played against each other, there was always an extra edge to the match. Neither team wanted to lose. So we ran faster, we tackled harder and we jumped higher than we normally would.

The Gorey Gladiators' captain – and my opposite number in the scrum – was Conor Kehoe. He was a really good hooker, as strong as an ox. But Conor's REAL talent was for mind games, which meant getting inside your head and putting you off your game.

There was one time when I was getting ready to throw the ball into the lineout and he sneaked up behind me – and pulled down my shorts!

That's right! I was left standing there looking like an idiot in just my underpants! After that, I couldn't throw the ball straight for the rest of the match, fearing that he was going to do it again.

It wasn't just *on* the field that he played these dirty tricks.

His dad had a fishmonger's called The Right Plaice in Kilmore Quay. One day, our team bus started to smell a bit funny. And when I say 'smell a bit funny', I mean it absolutely STANK. But for a whole year, our coach, Jimmy, couldn't find where the awful whiff was coming from. He thought it may have been a problem with the exhaust. He sent the bus to the best mechanics in Wexford, but none of them could discover the source of that terrible pong.

And so it remained a mystery – for a year. And during that year, the smell got worse and worse. Whenever we travelled to away matches, we were forced to cover our noses and mouths with our hands for the entire drive. Other times, the bus had to pull over so that some of the lads could be sick by the side of the road. Eventually, Jimmy had to issue the entire team with clothes pegs to put on our noses.

And then two weeks before we played the Gladiators in the final, we were on the way home from a match in Enniscorthy and got a puncture on the motorway. And that's when we finally discovered where the revolting smell was coming from. Jimmy lifted the trap door at the back of the bus to take out the spare tyre. And there, hidden underneath, was a plastic bag – filled with fish guts.

On the front of the bag, it said, 'The Right Plaice – Kilmore Quay'.

'Conor! Kehoe!' Jimmy declared, holding the bag at arm's length. 'That dirty little –'

I probably shouldn't tell you what words he used next. You could probably take a reasonable guess!

That not very funny 'joke' gave us an extra incentive to beat the Gorey Gladiators. That and the fact that it would be our last time ever playing together as a team.

After six years together, this was our last Wanderers outing, and I was a little bit sad on the way to the match. I was sitting at the back of the bus, next to Peter, and Gavin Eames, our kicker.

'It kind of feels like this is goodbye,' I said.

Gavin knew what I meant. In September, we were all going to start in different schools. Gavin was going to St Peter's, the local secondary.

'We'll stay in touch,' he said, although we all knew that, despite our best intentions, it probably wasn't true. We'd make new friends in our new schools. And by the time we met each other again, our Wexford Wanderers days would seem like a distant memory.

Peter would be going to Clongowes as well. Like me, he was looking forward to it, although for reasons *other* than rugby.

Peter was – and I mean this in the nicest possible way – a bit of a nerd. He wanted to be a doctor when he grew up and he already had his schoolbooks bought for next year.

'I don't even know if I'm going to be playing rugby next year,' he said as we pulled into the ground.

I couldn't believe what I was hearing.

'What are you talking about?' I said. 'We're going to Clongowes, Peter! It's going to be rugby, rugby, rugby – morning, noon and night!'

'Not for me,' he said. 'For me, it's going to be study, study, study – morning, noon and night. I'm going to need pretty much maximum points in my Leaving Certificate if I'm going to get into Medicine in Trinity College.'

'Well,' I said to Gavin and Peter, 'if this *is* going to be our last time playing together, let's make sure it's a match to remember.'

# 5  *A Match to Forget*

We got off the bus and headed straight for the dressing room, where Jimmy gave us what would be our last ever team talk.

'I've known you boys,' he said, 'since you were *that* high!' and he stuck out his hand to indicate that we'd been very, very small. 'You weren't much more than babies. And here you are now, all these years later, in the final of the Wexford Cup. This is a huge moment for you and for the club. I just want to let you know that, whatever happens today, I'm very proud of what you have achieved as a team. Remember, stick to the gameplan I gave you. And whatever you do, DON'T let that little so-and-so, Conor Kehoe, get inside your heads!'

Out we went onto the field. Mum and Dad were

standing on the sideline, alongside Ian, Shona and Megan.

'Good luck, Gordon!' they shouted.

And: 'Come on the Wanderers!'

The game kicked off.

The two teams were pretty evenly matched and there was no score at all after ten minutes. Then I managed to get my hands on the ball. I pulled it to my chest, slipped one tackle, then another, and suddenly a huge space seemed to open up in front of me. There was a roar from the crowd.

'Go on, Gordon!' they shouted. 'Keep going!'

I put my head down and ran in the direction of the line. I had about twenty metres to go. There were two Gorey players left to beat. One was their big number eight. He came running at me like the Wexford-to-Dublin train. I made a movement like I was about to pass the ball to my left. His eyes followed where he thought the ball was going. And that allowed me to switch direction, completely wrong-footing him.

'Brilliant!' Jimmy shouted. 'The boy's a genius!'

Now, I just had their full-back to beat. He was a big lad. Again, he came rushing out to meet me. He was unlikely to fall for the same trick as his teammate, I thought. So instead of trying to sell him a dummy, I kicked the ball ahead of me. I hit it right on the sweet spot. The ball went one side of him and I went around the other.

The crowd roared with excitement.

The ball hit the ground right in front of the posts and bounced up into the air. I anticipated exactly where it was going to go. I jumped and caught it perfectly. Then I dived over the line and grounded the ball.

Everyone went crazy as my teammates congratulated me.

'Did you see what that kid just did?' I heard them ask.

I thought we had it made then, but that's when things started to go wrong.

A short time later, we won a scrum. It was the first time in the match that I came face-to-face with Conor. He smiled at me as the two sets of forwards moved into place and awaited the referee's instructions.

'Crouch!' he said.

And we crouched.

'Pause!' he said.

Then we paused.

'Touch!' he said.

So we touched.

'Engage!' he said.

And we engaged.

I felt the weight of Conor's shoulder against mine as we each tried to force the other to take a backwards step. And then, out of nowhere, Conor said in my ear:

'Hey, I heard *fishious* rumours about a terrible smell on your team bus!'

It sort of threw me for a moment that he would say something like that and I was forced to take a step backwards.

'We *know* it was you,' I told him as I tried to push back, 'who put that bag of fish guts under the spare tyre!'

He didn't budge.

'For Heaven's *hake*,' he said, 'put some *mussel* into it!'

Peter put the ball in, then he raced around to the back of the scrum to wait for me to hook it back to him. But Conor was getting inside my head with his fish puns.

'You think you're hilarious,' I said, my shoulder straining against his.

'Hey, *clam* down!' he replied. 'I'm just saying that this is *dolphin*-itely not the time or the *plaice* to start bringing it up!'

And in that moment, I laughed. I couldn't help myself. But I also lost my concentration and their front row was able to push us back far enough for Conor to steal the ball.

And it kept happening like that – over and over and over again.

'What's going on?' Peter eventually asked me. 'We haven't won a single scrum today!'

'It's that Conor lad!' I told him. 'He keeps making jokes about what he did to our bus!'

'Jimmy told you not to let him inside your head!' Peter reminded me.

But I *had* let him inside. And inside he stayed for the entire match. I had to listen to him slagging me every time I got my hands on the ball.

Once, when I was getting ready to throw the ball into the lineout, he shouted, 'You've got a great throw, Gordon – there's no *trout* about it!'

I threw a crooked ball and the Gorey Gladiators stole it from us.

Or when I got the ball in my hands and I tried to gain some ground for us, he shouted, 'That's it, Gordon, get your *skates* on! Don't leave it to *salmon* else!'

Despite my try, I ended up having a terrible match. With five minutes to go, we were losing by 15–10 and we needed a converted try to win. The referee blew for a scrum right on their twenty-two and once again we had the put-in.

Peter pulled me to one side.

'Gordon, this is it,' he said. 'This is our last chance to win the cup! Just shut his voice out of your head and focus, okay?'

We crouched. We touched. We paused. We engaged.

'This is it, fellas!' Conor announced. 'This is your last oppor-*tuna*-ty to score!'

But this time I refused to let it throw me. As a matter of fact, it just made me angry. And that anger seemed to give me some kind of super-human strength . . . which allowed me to push Conor and the rest of the Gorey scrum back one step . . .

Then another . . .

Then another . . .

Now, the ball was right under my feet. But instead of hooking it towards the back of the scrum, I kept rolling it forward under my foot.

And the Gorey scrum continued to move, until suddenly we were shunting them back towards their own tryline.

Conor wasn't laughing anymore.

'PUSH, FELLAS!' he was suddenly shouting. 'PUT YOUR WEIGHT INTO IT!'

Behind me, I could hear Peter shouting, 'GIVE ME THE BALL! GIVE ME THE BALL!' so he could feed it to our backs to have a run at the line.

But I kept rolling it forward . . .

And rolling it forward . . .

And rolling it forward . . .

Until I discovered that we were very, very near to the Gorey tryline.

'PUSH, FELLAS!' Conor was shouting. 'PUSH, FELLAS!'

But such was our momentum that we couldn't be stopped. A second or two later, I looked down and saw that we'd crossed the Gorey tryline.

I immediately took my arms off the shoulders of my front-row teammates and fell on top of the ball.

The referee blew his whistle and signalled a try!

We were now level with the Gorey Gladiators, with the conversion still to come. If Gavin could put the ball between the sticks, then the cup was ours. And it wasn't a difficult kick because I'd touched the ball down right under the posts.

I threw the ball to Gavin and he placed it in the cup, right in front of the goal. Then he took four steps backwards and three to the side.

'Just take your time, Gavin!' I said. 'Focus on the posts.'

And that's when Conor piped up again.

'That's right, Gavin!' he said. 'You were *prawn* to do this!'

'Don't listen to him!' I tried to tell him. 'Don't lose your focus!'

Gavin started his run-up.

And that's when Conor shouted: 'You're *codding* yourself if you think you can score from there!'

All of the Gorey Gladiators players laughed.

And Gavin mis-hit the ball . . .

And it skewed sideways off his boot . . .

And it flew off to the right . . .

And out of play . . .

And seconds later, the referee blew the final whistle and declared the match . . .

A DRAW!

We all fell to our knees with our heads in our hands. The cup was going to be . . . shared.

We had come so close to winning, it felt like a loss to us. There were no hugs, no high-fives, just a horrible silence. I was so crushed, I didn't even feel like staying around for the presentation. But Jimmy persuaded me that it was the right thing to do.

'You're not going to win every match,' he said. 'Trust me — there'll be many, many days like this one.'

So I went up to receive the trophy on behalf of the Wexford Wanderers. And Conor Kehoe went up to receive it on behalf of the Gorey Gladiators.

The referee said, 'Here you go, lads,' handing it over.

We each took a handle.

'I'm happy to declare,' the referee said, 'that the result of this year's Wexford Cup final is – a draw!'

And we both held the trophy up above our heads.

I gritted my teeth in anger.

'You cheated!' I said.

But Conor just laughed and said, 'I'm *herring* a lot of anger from you, Gordon!'

# 6  *Leaving Home*

All that summer, my friends kept teasing me about going to boarding school, telling me I'd be crying into my pillow every night and dying to get back to Wexford. Normally, I'd have been wishing the summer holidays would go on forever, but not this time. All I wanted to do was play rugby. And I knew that when I got to Clongowes, I would be playing rugby all day, every day.

I wished away the summer months so that I could start school in September.

Mum and Dad didn't even have to wake me the morning we were supposed to drive to Kildare.

Mum was shouting up the stairs, 'Gordon D'Arcy, if you don't get out of that bed now, I won't be responsible for my actions!'

But I was already sitting in the back seat of the

car, dressed in my school uniform, with my brand-new Clongowes rugby jersey on underneath. It had purple and white horizontal stripes and the school crest embroidered on it and a thick white collar, which I turned inside-out so it wouldn't show over my school shirt.

Inside the house, I could hear Dad upstairs, yelling, 'Gordon D'Arcy, your mother has called you three times already!' And then there was a moment's pause. 'He's not here! He's not in his bed! Oh dear God, he's run away from home!'

I leaned forward between the two front seats of the car and I pressed down impatiently on the horn.

BEEEPPP!!!    BEEEPPP!!!    BEEEPPP!!! BEEEPPP!!!

A moment later, Dad appeared at the front door.

'It's okay,' he shouted to Mum, 'he's already in the car! Where are your bags, Gordon?'

'In the boot!' I said. 'Come on, let's go!'

I was *very* impatient to get on the road.

The rest of the family emerged from the house. They were coming along for the drive. Dad locked the front door, while Ian got into the front passenger seat. Shona, Megan and Mum squeezed into the back seat with me.

'I suppose we should be pleased that you're so

keen to go to school,' Mum said, kissing the top of my head.

Dad started the car and we were off to Kildare. I had butterflies in my stomach.

'How long will it take to get there?' I asked.

'About two hours,' Dad said.

'Not if you REALLY put your foot down, Dad.'

'We'll get there when we get there, Gordon!'

Once we got onto the main road, Shona took out the *Clongowes Wood College Guidebook for New Students* and read it from cover to cover, quoting lines from it every now and then.

'You know you're going to be attending the same school as James Joyce?' she said.

'What position did he play?' I asked.

'Er, he's the author of *Ulysses*,' she explained. 'It's one of the most important books EVER written.'

'But did he play rugby for the school?' I said.

'I don't think so. It doesn't say it here.'

'That's probably why no one's ever heard of him, then.'

Ian laughed. 'There's more to life in boarding school than just playing rugby,' he said. Ian had finished school and would soon be starting college. 'Hey, everyone, Gordon's got his rugby gear on underneath his uniform.'

They all thought that was HILARIOUS!

All except Megan. She was very upset about having to say goodbye to me.

'Will we ever see him again?' she wanted to know.

'Of course,' Mum said. 'He'll be home in four weeks.'

'FOUR WEEKS?' she screamed. 'THAT'S AGES AWAY!'

'The time will fly,' Mum assured her.

After what seemed like the longest journey EVER, we finally reached the school. Somewhere in the middle of the Kildare countryside, we took a left turn and found ourselves driving through a set of enormous, black gates. Then we drove up a driveway that was so long, it felt like we would never reach the end of it.

I was staring at the rugby pitches to my left. I was so fixated on them that I didn't even see the castle until it was right in front of us.

It was HUGE – like something a king and queen would live in.

'Is this it?' I asked.

'Impressive, huh?' said Ian.

'It doesn't look like a school,' I said. 'It looks like, I don't know, Dracula's house.'

I noticed a lot of other cars pulling up beside us. And lots of boys my age were staring up in wonder at the building, just like me.

'That's what I was trying to tell you,' Shona said. 'There's a lot of history attached to the place. It's nearly two hundred years old!'

I was already taking off my school jumper as I was getting out of the car. Dad cleared his throat in an embarrassed way.

'Er, Gordon,' he said, 'like Ian was saying, I

don't think you're going to be playing rugby *straight away*.'

'Really?' I said. 'Why not?'

'First, they're going to show you to your room,' Ian said. 'Then there'll be some kind of assembly for all the new boys. They call it Induction. It's to help you get settled in.'

Dad helped me take my bags out of the boot.

'Well, this is it!' said Mum in a sad voice – now *she* was the one who was talking like it was the last time we were ever going to see each other. 'Are you absolutely SURE this is what you want?'

'Mum,' I said, 'I'm excited!'

I gave her a big hug. Then I hugged Dad, Ian, Shona and lastly Megan, who really didn't want me to go and wrapped herself around my leg until Ian and Shona gently prised her off me.

They got back into the car, waved at me, then drove away.

I have to admit to being just the tiniest bit nervous at the thought of being on my own for the first time in my life. I looked up at that huge castle with its grey stone walls and its pointed windows and its turreted roof . . .

. . . and I gulped.

Like this:

GUUULP!!!

But then I gathered myself, picked up my bags and walked through the big front doors.

Standing inside was a very tall man with red hair. In his hand was the biggest bunch of keys I had ever seen – like something a jailer might carry around with him.

'My name is Mr Cuffe,' he said, 'and I am the Principal of Clongowes Wood College. The dormitories where you will sleep are down the corridor to my left. Each dormitory sleeps four students in two sets of bunk beds. One bed per boy. If you have trouble finding a dormitory, return to me and I will assign one to you.'

I was wondering had Peter arrived yet. I walked down the long corridor, looking around doors as I went. Behind some, there was laughter and excitement – boys who were thrilled to be setting off on this new adventure. Behind others, there were boys sitting in silence or, worse, sobbing. I realized that not everyone was as happy to be here as I was.

I walked to the end of the corridor, and that's when I heard a voice that I knew so well.

'If you must know, I'm reading about the human respiratory system. I don't wish to be rude, but I'll need an A in Biology if I'm going to be a doctor.'

I had a little chuckle to myself. It was typical Peter. But who was he talking to? I wondered.

I pushed the door open, then I just stood there, rooted to the spot, in shock.

Peter was sitting at the study desk, his nose buried in his Biology book. And lying on the bottom bunk opposite me, with his hands behind his head, was my arch-enemy . . .

Conor Kehoe!

# 7 The Same Side

'What are *you* doing here?' I said.

Conor sat up on the bed. 'What do you mean?' he asked. 'I'm boarding here – just like you!'

'I didn't know you were coming to this school,' I said.

He shrugged. 'It's a great rugby school,' he said. 'I want to learn from the legendary Vinnie Murray.'

'Well,' I said, picking up his bags, 'you are NOT staying in this room.'

Peter looked up from his book. 'I told him you wouldn't be happy,' he said.

'Why not?' Conor asked – like he didn't know!

'Because you put a bag of fish guts on our team bus!' I reminded him. '*And* you pulled my shorts down when I was about to throw the ball into the lineout! *And* you shouted jokes at Gavin to put him off his kick in the final!'

Conor grinned. 'Ah, come on,' he said, 'you're not a Wexford Wanderer anymore. And I'm not a Gorey Gladiator.'

Then he opened the top two buttons of his shirt. Underneath, he was wearing his Clongowes jersey – just like me.

'We're both on the same side now,' he said.

But I shook my head. 'We are definitely NOT on the same side!' I told him. 'And we never will be!'

I put his bags outside the door.

He shook his head. 'We're Clongowes now, Gordon,' he said. 'And we're both Wexford men, that means we should stick together. We held that cup together, remember. There's nothing to argue about now.'

'You didn't deserve that cup,' I said. 'That was dirty tactics and you know it.'

'Well, then, you should want me to be on your side,' Conor said with a grin, 'rather than working against you.'

He kind of had a point. Maybe.

'Look, to tell you the truth,' he said, 'I'm a little bit homesick here. And I don't know a single person in the school – except you two fellas.'

'The only reason you *know* us,' I reminded him, 'is because you CHEATED us out of the Wexford Cup!'

'Gordon,' he said, 'I play to my strengths, just like you play to yours. You're a better hooker than me. Slightly – there wouldn't be a lot in it. So I used whatever tactics I had to even up the contest.'

'What, like making jokes to put me off?'

'I never played better than when I played against you, Gordon. And, if you were honest with yourself, you'd say that you never played better than when you played against me. Whatever you think of me, we brought out the best in each other.'

He made his way to the door and picked up his bags. His shoulders were hunched like he'd just been hit by a ferocious tackle. He looked a bit defeated, and it didn't suit him.

'Wait!' I said.

He turned around and I looked at him, standing in the doorway, holding his bags, looking sad.

'You're right,' I told him. 'You did make me want to be a better player.' I smiled at him. 'So put your things in the wardrobe there.'

'You mean I can stay?' he asked.

'Yes, you can stay,' I said, 'provided it's okay with Peter.'

Peter looked up from his book. 'Yeah,' he said, 'can you two keep the noise down? The summer exams are only nine months away.'

I stuck out my hand. Conor dropped his bags and we shook on it. And, looking back, that was the moment when we went from being sworn enemies to being sort of friends.

A moment later, a voice came over the P.A. system, saying: 'ALL BOYS TO APPEAR IN THE MAIN ASSEMBLY HALL IN SIXTY SECONDS! ALL BOYS TO APPEAR IN THE MAIN ASSEMBLY HALL IN SIXTY SECONDS!'

Peter stood up, took his blazer off the back of the chair and put it on. 'That'll be the Induction,' he said. 'Come on, we don't want to be late.'

Like everything else in Clongowes, the main assembly hall was ENORMOUS. I shuffled in with Conor, Peter and all the other new boys, most of us complete strangers to each other. There were no chairs set out in the hall and we all had to stand in a series of rows, facing the stage. Peter insisted we go right to the very front.

71

There was a low, excited murmur in the room while we waited. Then a priest walked out onto the stage and said his name was Father Billings. He was very old.

'My God,' Conor whispered out of the corner of his mouth, 'this fella looks like he was alive when the Bible was written!'

Behind us, a few boys laughed. But I was staring at the walls, which were covered with photographs of all the rugby teams who'd done the school proud down through the years.

I remembered Ian telling me that Father Billings was almost completely deaf, which meant he had to shout to hear his own voice.

'GOOD MORNING, BOYS!' he bellowed. 'AND WELCOME TO YOUR NEW LIFE AT CLONGOWES WOOD COLLEGE! I HOPE THAT YOUR YEARS SPENT HERE WILL PROVE BENEFICIAL TO YOUR INTEL-LECTUAL, SPIRITUAL AND PERSONAL GROWTH!'

The other thing that Father Billings was – apart from almost completely deaf – was prone to farting. He was very, VERY prone to farting. But his deaf-ness meant he was completely unaware of this fact.

'WE HERE AT CLONGOWES WOOD

ARE JUSTLY PROUD OF THE RECORD
OF OUR PAST PUPILS IN THE AREAS OF
BUSINESS, POLITICS, RUGBY AND THE
ARTS ...'

And that's when it happened:

*PHHHFFFAAARRRTTT!!!*

The noise ripped through the assembly hall. All
of the boys laughed. Standing behind him on the
stage, Mr Cuffe rattled his enormous collection of
keys as a warning to us to behave ourselves.

Father Billings continued to talk at the top of his
voice: 'OUR PAST PUPILS HAVE INCLUDED

FAMOUS WRITERS, JUDGES, BUSINESS-
MEN, SPORTSMEN, GOVERNMENT
MINISTERS AND ONE TAOISEACH . . .'

The next one was even LOUDER and it went on
for AGES:

*PHHHHHAAAAARRRRRTTTTT!!!!!*

We all tried not to laugh this time. But it was a
struggle. I thought I might burst trying to hold it in.

'Did you say your name was *Father* Billings,'
Conor shouted, 'or *Farter* Billings?'

I laughed at that. We all did. Mr Cuffe shot us all
an angry look and rattled his keys again.

Father Billings smiled and said: 'IT'S WON-
DERFUL TO SEE A GROUP OF STUDENTS
WITH SMILING FACES! HONESTLY, MR
CUFFE, I THINK THE FIRST YEARS GET
HAPPIER AND HAPPIER EVERY YEAR.'

*PPPPPPHHHHHHHFFFFFFAAAAAAR-
RRRRRTTTTTT!!!!!!!*

I was laughing so much now that I was struggling
to breathe.

'NOW, I'M GOING TO INVITE MR
CUFFE, THE PRINCIPAL, TO EXPLAIN
TO YOU HOW THE TIMETABLE
WORKS HERE AT CLONGOWES WOOD
COLLEGE.'

Mr Cuffe stepped forward.

'During the course of the next six years of your lives,' Mr Cuffe said, 'you are going to become VERY familiar with bells!'

We all looked at each other with confused faces.

'Bells?' I said to Peter. 'He must have meant balls. He's obviously talking about rugby.'

But he WASN'T talking about rugby!

'A *bell*,' Mr Cuffe continued, 'will wake you up at 7.30 a.m. to tell you that it's time to get out of your lazy beds and get yourselves washed and dressed for the day. A bell will sound at 8.10 a.m. to tell you that it's time to go to morning study. A bell will sound at 8.55 a.m. to tell you that it's time to go to your first class of the morning, which will be DOUBLE MATHS . . .'

'*Double* maths?' Peter said, mainly to himself. 'I'm wondering is double enough? Does that not seem a bit short to you?'

'A bell will sound at 10.15 a.m. to tell you that it's time to go to your next class, which will be DOUBLE HISTORY. A bell will sound at 11.35 a.m. to tell you that it's time to go to your next class, which will be DOUBLE PHYSICS . . .'

I couldn't believe what I was hearing – even though Ian *had* tried to warn me. I thought I was going to some kind of rugby academy. Now, it seems, I was expected to do *actual* schoolwork – and a lot of schoolwork, from the way Mr Cuffe was talking.

'This isn't a school!' I said quietly to Conor. 'It's a prison!'

'WHAT ABOUT RUGBY?' Conor shouted.

'Who said that?' Mr Cuffe asked.

Conor put up his hand.

'It was me, Sir,' he replied. 'I'm sorry to have to bring this up, but I was led to believe that we were going to be playing a lot of rugby.'

'Were you, indeed?' said Mr Cuffe.

And then, right on cue, the door behind us opened and Mr Cuffe said: 'Ah, Mr Murray! We were just talking about you!'

Silence descended on the assembly hall. All whispering and fidgeting and giggling stopped as we listened to the sound of his footsteps behind us. Then, a moment later, he was standing in front of us on the stage – a tall man with grey hair and glasses.

'Hello, everyone,' he said. 'My name is Mr Murray.'

We all stood there in silent awe. Everyone knew that this man was a legend.

'So,' he said, 'are any of you boys interested in rugby?'

Conor was the first to reply.

'ER, DOES THE WEXFORD WANDER-ERS' TEAM BUS SMELL OF FISH?' he shouted. Then he turned to me and said, 'Sorry, Gordon, couldn't resist it.'

'What about the rest of you?' Mr Murray asked.

'YES!' we all shouted as one.

'Yes, what?'

'YES, MR MURRAY!'

'Good,' he said. 'You have one hour of Free Time between 4.00 p.m. and 5.00 p.m. each day. And on Mondays and Wednesdays, at that time, I take the First Years for rugby training.'

'Yes!' I said, punching the air.

'But a word of warning,' he said. 'Clongowes Wood College is a school, not a rugby academy. While we have had lots of success on the field, play-ing rugby is a privilege that will be extended to those of you who work hard at your schoolwork. I'll see you all tomorrow.'

Then he walked out of the room. There was a low murmur among the boys. Most of us were just say-ing, 'Vinnie Murray! Wow!'

'And speaking of schoolwork,' Mr Cuffe said,

returning to the subject of our daily class schedule, 'a bell will sound at 5.30 p.m. to tell you that it's time for Evening Study . . .'

But I was already thinking about rugby training at 4.00 p.m. tomorrow. And all I could hear coming out of Mr Cuffe's mouth was: 'Blah, blah, blah, blah, blah, blah, blah.'

# 8 Flash Barry

I had real trouble falling asleep that night – my first as a boarder in Clongowes Wood College. It had nothing to do with my excitement about training under the legendary Vinnie Murray the following day. Nor did it have anything to do with Peter's snoring – although he WAS a loud snorer. This is how it sounded:

HOOOCCCKKK . . . ZZZUUUUUU!!!!!!

No, the reason I couldn't get to sleep was because Conor tossed and turned so violently in his sleep, I kept being thrown from the bed.

And I was in the *top* bunk, remember?

One minute, I was just drifting off, then the next . . .

AAARRRGGGHHH!!!

I woke up to find myself falling face-forward towards the floor, then hitting it with a . . .

BUUUMMMPPP!!!

After the fourth time it happened, I shook Conor awake.

'Conor,' I said, 'you're going to have to swap beds with me.'

'What?' he asked, clearly oblivious to what had been happening. 'Why?'

'I've fallen off the bed four times now,' I told him, 'with all your tossing and turning. At least if I sleep in the lower bunk, I'll have a shorter distance to fall.'

'I can't sleep in the top bunk,' Conor said. 'I toss and turn in my sleep.'

'Yeah,' I said, 'I've kind of *noticed* that!'

'Well, *I* don't want to keep falling out of the top bunk, do I? Why don't you sleep above Peter there?'

I hadn't actually thought of that. The fourth bed in our dorm – the other top bunk – was still empty. We'd been told that a boy named Barry would be arriving either that night or the following morning.

'You should claim that bed before the other lad gets here,' Conor said.

But no sooner had he spoken the words than the door swung open, the light was switched on and in walked a tall, thin boy wearing wraparound shades – even though it was almost midnight.

'Hey, guys!' he said. 'How the hell are you?'

He was from somewhere in Dublin and he talked VERY differently from us. For instance, he called us 'guys' instead of 'lads'.

He threw his bag on the bunk above Peter's – my plan foiled.

'You must be Barry,' I said.

'You better believe I'm Barry!' he said, removing his wraparound shades. 'They call me Flash Barry. Or just Flash for short.'

'It's, er, nice to meet you.'

'What accent is that I'm hearing?'

'Wexford,' Conor said. 'We're all from Wexford in this room.'

'Wexford?' Barry asked, laughing to himself. 'Wait'll they hear about this at home! They'll think that's hilarious! Wexford!'

'I'm Gordon,' I told him.

'I'm Conor,' Conor said. 'And that fella in the bunk below you asleep is Peter.'

HOOOCCCKKK . . . ZZZUUUUUU!!!!!!

'He's a serious snorer,' Barry said, 'isn't he?'

He didn't say it was nice to meet us or anything like that. Instead, he rolled up his sleeve to show us his watch. It was the biggest watch I'd ever seen and it looked ridiculous on his tiny wrist.

'Check this out,' he said. 'It's a diver's watch. This

baby is the last word in robust, go-anywhere time-keeping. It provides an illuminated numerical display that's accurate to the millisecond and it's water-resistant to a depth of three hundred metres.'

Conor smiled and said, 'Have you a very deep bath at home or something?'

Barry stared at him, with no expression, for about twenty seconds. Then he smiled.

'Okay,' he said, 'you're obviously the funny man. Do you want to hit me in the stomach?'

'Do I want to what?' Conor asked.

Barry slapped his belly twice.

'My stomach,' he said. 'It's as hard as that wall there. What about you, Norman?'

'Gordon,' I reminded him.

'Gordon, then. Do you want to have a go? Hit me as hard as you can. I swear to God, I won't feel a thing.'

'But wouldn't I hurt my hand,' I asked, 'if it's as hard as that wall?'

'You're absolutely right!' he said. 'You WOULD hurt your hand!'

'I think I'll pass, then.'

'If you change your mind, the offer stands!'

'I'll, er, keep that in mind.'

He stared at Peter, still in a deep sleep.

HOOOCCCKKK . . . ZZZUUUUUU!!!!!!

Using the sole of his foot, Barry shook the mattress until Peter woke up.

'What's going on?' he asked, sitting bolt upright in the bed. 'Is it time for class? Am I late?'

'I'm Barry,' Barry said. 'And if you insist on snoring like that, me and you are definitely NOT going to get along.'

He climbed up onto the bunk above Peter and lay down with his fingers knotted behind his head.

Suddenly, one of the Sixth Year prefects appeared at the door.

'What's all the noise in here?' he asked.

'Conor keeps tossing and turning in his sleep,' I told him, 'and I keep falling out of the bed.'

The prefect laughed. 'There's always one,' he said, 'every year.'

He disappeared out of the dorm, then reappeared a few minutes later, holding a hammer, a box of nails and several lengths of wood.

'Where did you get those?' I asked.

'The caretaker's workshop,' he answered.

'What are you going to do with them?' I wondered.

'Watch,' he told me.

Then he set to work. He nailed the wooden planks

to the bed. One on the right side and one on the left side. Then he nailed another one to the head of the bed and another to the foot of the bed. So that my bed suddenly looked like . . .

. . . an open coffin.

I remembered that the school looked like Dracula's castle. I couldn't help but laugh.

'You definitely won't fall out of bed now!' Conor said.

I climbed up the ladder, swung one leg over the wooden side, then the other and slipped under the covers.

'We'd better get some sleep,' I said. 'Tomorrow is a big day.'

'I know,' Peter agreed. 'Double Maths, then Double History, then Double Physics. Clongowes is everything I hoped it would be and more!'

'I think Gordon was actually talking about rugby training,' Conor said.

And Barry said: 'Now, if you guys wouldn't mind letting me get some sleep – I want to impress this Vinnie Murray guy tomorrow.'

# 9 *Centre of Attention*

I daydreamed my way through Double Maths the following morning. And through Double History. And through Double Physics.

As a matter of fact, I fell asleep during Double Physics. When I woke up, Mr McManus, the teacher, was staring at me, asking me a question about angular velocity, which I was in no position to answer since I'd spent the last twenty minutes in Dreamland.

I could even feel dribble on my chin.

Thankfully, Peter saved my skin.

'The up-or-down orientation of angular velocity,' he blurted out, 'is conventionally specified by the right-hand rule, Sir!'

Mr McManus said, 'Very good – but please don't answer unless I ask YOU a question specifically!'

Then he turned around and started writing on the board.

I looked at Peter and whispered, 'Thanks.'

'That's okay,' he said. 'You should maybe try to stay awake, though.'

The day passed slowly. But eventually four o'clock came around and we headed for the rugby field – me, Conor and Peter, with Barry tagging along behind us.

There were about forty of us packed into the dressing room, changing into our purple and white striped jerseys and our rugby boots, the excitement building.

Outside on the pitch, Mr Murray was waiting for us. At his feet were two piles of high-viz vests – one lot yellow, the other lot orange.

'Everyone grab a vest!' he said.

Wexford people are sometimes known as the Yellow Bellies and that was the reason I chose yellow. Barry picked up a yellow vest, too. But Conor and Peter chose orange. We pulled them on over our jerseys.

'Okay,' Mr Murray said, 'the yellows are one team and the oranges are another. I want to organize you into two lots of backs and forwards so I can see what kind of skills you have.'

Then he started pointing out boys individually.

'The tall guy there,' he said, 'you're going to be in the second row. And so's your friend beside you . . . you're going to be a full-back . . . you there, you're going to be a winger.'

He pointed at me and said, 'You're going to play at inside-centre.'

'The thing is,' I told him, 'I'm usually a hooker – like Keith Wood.'

'I don't care what you *usually* are,' he said. 'Today, I want to see you play centre.'

'Yes, Sir.'

Barry was told he was to play on the left wing. Conor was told to play hooker for the orange team and Peter was told to play in his usual scrum-half position.

Mr Murray blew the whistle and the match got under way.

It was all a bit chaotic, though. No one was really playing as part of a team. Everyone was too keen to show Mr Murray what they were capable of – especially Barry. Whenever he got the ball, he refused to pass it to anyone.

We'd been playing for about twenty minutes when I started to get to grips with the game. I was beating players and pinging passes around. I was really surprised at how much I was enjoying being a back rather than a forward.

My teammates started giving me the ball every chance they got, looking to me to make something happen. And I started thinking, maybe the coach is right. Maybe I *am* a centre after all.

During a break in play, Mr Murray looked at me through narrowed eyes and said, 'What's your name?'

'It's, em, Gordon D'Arcy,' I said, nervously.

'Ian's brother!' he said, nodding, as if this confirmed something he'd already been thinking.

'Yes, Sir.'

But then he didn't say anything else. So I didn't know whether he was impressed with me or not.

A few minutes later, I received a pass from a boy whose name I didn't know yet and I set off on a run. I beat one player . . .

Then another . . .

Then another . . .

Then . . .

BANG!

Suddenly, I found myself lying on the ground, feeling like a tree had just fallen on me. When my head cleared, I realized that I'd been tackled by Conor.

'Just keeping you honest,' he said, holding out his hand to help me up.

I had to laugh.

In the second half, I had the ball again and Conor tried to repeat the trick. This time, I saw him out of the corner of my eye. With a flick of my hips, I slipped the tackle, then I kicked the ball into the space behind the opposition. Barry seemed to read my mind and he raced onto it and gathered it up.

He had his finger in the air before he even crossed the tryline. He performed a spectacular swan dive before grounding the ball. Then he put his two hands in the air and shouted, 'Remember this moment! All of you! That includes you, Mr Murray!'

I could suddenly see why they called him Flash Barry.

It was the only try of the game and the stand-out moment of the day. When the final whistle blew, most of the boys on my team rushed to congratulate Barry, whose quick thinking had won the match for us.

Conor said, 'He, er, kind of loves himself, doesn't he?'

I noticed that Barry was inviting our teammates to punch him in the stomach.

We started to walk back to the dressing rooms.

'He's definitely not a team player,' Peter said. 'Although I'd say the coach was impressed.'

But Mr Murray didn't pay him any attention. Instead, he walked over to me and he said, 'That kick of yours – the one that led to the try . . .'

'What was wrong with it?' I asked, convinced that I'd done something wrong.

'Why did you choose to kick it?' he asked. 'I mean, it was a long shot that that boy was going to get to it. You had two players outside you. If you'd passed the ball to one of them, it would have been a certain try.'

'I was worried about the intercept,' I told him.

'The intercept?'

'Yeah, I could see one of their players anticipating

the pass, so I decided that there was less of a risk in kicking it.'

'Interesting,' he said.

But that was *all* he said. Just:

'Interesting.'

What did that mean? I had no idea.

# 10  *Bowled Over*

'What do you think he meant?'

I was still pondering the question twenty-four hours later.

'What are you talking about?' Conor asked.

'When he said what I did with the ball was *interesting*,' I said. 'I mean, did he mean *interesting* in a good way or a bad way?'

We were throwing the ball back and forth to each other in the car park.

'In a good way,' Conor assured me.

'Definitely?' I asked.

'Definitely! You played great, Gordon! You were the Man of the Match!'

'I don't know about that. Everyone's still talking about Barry's try.'

'Barry isn't a team player, though. Barry plays for

Barry. Trust me, Vinnie was impressed with you . . .
OOPS!'

He accidentally overthrew a pass. I had to run
backwards at high speed in order to reach it. And
that's how I ended up knocking over someone who
happened to be walking past.

'Oh God, I'm sorry,' I said, turning around.

I looked down and saw that it was a girl – which I
wasn't expecting in the grounds of a boarding school
for boys.

'You're . . . a girl!' I said.

'Very observant of you to notice,' she replied. 'Are

you going to help me up or are you just going to stand there with your stupid mouth open?'

I reached out my hand and I helped her up.

Conor laughed. 'Gordon,' he said, 'this is my cousin, Aoife. She's in St Bridget's.'

St Bridget's was a boarding school for girls across the road from Clongowes.

'Aoife,' Conor said, 'this is my friend, Gordon.'

She just stared at me. And not in a friendly way.

'Your friend Gordon should really watch where he's going,' she said.

I apologized again. Then she turned to Conor.

'I just called over to see did you have a kicking tee I could borrow?' she said.

'A kicking tee?' I asked. I may have even laughed. 'Why would *you* want one of those?'

'To practise my kicking!' she said in a matter-of-fact way. 'Why would *anyone* want a kicking tee?'

'Seriously, though?'

'What, you mean you've never met a girl who played rugby before?'

'Er, no,' I said – because the truth was, I hadn't. 'Anyway, Conor, we better head back inside. Free Time is nearly over.'

I took about ten steps. Then, suddenly, without any warning, I felt the air leave my lungs, and something hard hit me in the head. It turned out to be the ground.

Conor's cousin had tackled me around the waist and dumped me face-down on the asphalt.

My God, I thought! She tackles even harder than Conor!

Actually, she tackled even harder than Ian!

I rolled over onto my back and managed to lift myself up onto my elbows. I was still winded and my head felt light.

'So you've never met a girl who played rugby before?' she said, as she climbed to her feet again. 'Well, congratulations, Gordon – you have now!'

# 11  *The Night of the Big, BIG Trouble*

The months passed. I settled into life at Clongowes Wood. I grew used to the endless bells marking out my days. I was really enjoying my rugby on Monday and Wednesday afternoons. So, too, were Conor and Peter – and, of course, Flash Barry, who had made the swan-dive finish his trademark move.

I played my very best at every training session, but I still didn't know if Mr Murray rated me as a player. He would ask me questions about certain decisions I'd made on the pitch. Why did I pass to this player instead of that player? Why did I cut inside with the ball when there was a clear channel down the left? Why did I choose to offload the ball when I had a chance of scoring a try myself in the corner?

I always explained the reasons behind my decisions to him – and he always said, 'Interesting.'

And never anything more than that.

I was also getting on well with my schoolwork – although obviously not as well as Peter, who was top of the class in every subject.

Every three or four weekends, I went home to Wexford to see Mum and Dad and Ian and Shona and Megan. It was always great to see them, but I really LOVED going back to school once the weekend was over.

And, yes, I know that makes me sound like a strange kid!

Life was good. And then, shortly after the Christmas holidays, I did something that, in a roundabout way, was to change my entire life.

It started off like any other night. I was having difficulty sleeping because of the sound of Peter's snoring. It was the usual:

HOOOCCCKKK . . . ZZZUUUUUU!!!!!!

It was the early hours of the morning and I was wide awake, staring at the ceiling of the dormitory and thinking about rugby. That's when I heard a voice say:

'Is anyone else awake?'

It was Conor.

'Yeah,' I said, 'I can't sleep because of that noise.'

HOOOCCCKKK . . . ZZZUUUUUU!!!!!!

'Me neither,' said Barry.

'Let's get up,' Conor suggested, 'and play some pranks!'

I sat up in my coffin.

'Pranks?' I said.

HOOOCCCKKK . . . ZZZUUUUUU!!!!!!

'Yeah,' he said, 'you know how Farter Billings is always saying it's a sin to waste a single minute of our time here in school? Well, wasting time is what we're doing right now! We should get up and do something productive.'

Maybe I should have said no. But after a moment of thought . . .

HOOOCCCKKK . . . ZZZUUUUUU!!!!!!

. . . I said, 'Okay, it's better than lying here and listening to that!'

So I climbed out of my coffin as quietly as I could. At the same time, Conor and Barry got out of their beds.

'I already have an idea,' Conor said.

He took three thick, black marker pens from the drawer of his study desk.

'Let's draw moustaches on all the other boys while they're asleep!' he said.

Barry and I had to put our hands over our mouths to stop ourselves from laughing.

This . . . was . . . genius!

Conor handed us each a marker and we crept out of the dorm and went to work.

'What kind of moustaches should we give them?' I asked.

'Let's do all different ones!' Conor suggested.

'Conor,' Barry said, 'that is absolutely brilliant!'

So that's what we did.

On the faces of some boys, we drew handlebar moustaches . . .

On the faces of some boys, we drew pencil moustaches – and very distinguished they looked in them, too . . .

On the faces of other boys, we drew horseshoe moustaches . . .

On the faces of some boys, we drew paintbrush moustaches . . .

And on other boys, we drew big, bushy walrus moustaches.

It took about two hours of silently creeping around the dormitories before we had given every First Year boy asleep in the school a very fetching set of whiskers.

Then, giggling to ourselves, we returned to our room. Conor and Barry got back into their beds and I returned to my coffin. Peter was still fast asleep.

HOOOCCCKKK . . . ZZZUUUUUU!!!!!!

We all drifted off.

We were awoken by the sound of titters, then giggles, then outright howls of laughter from the rooms up and down the corridor.

'You've got a moustache!' one boy would say.

Then the other would reply, 'No, *you're* the one with the moustache!'

A few moments later, I heard Mr Cuffe's voice in the hallway outside. He was shouting:

'WHAT IN THE NAME OF GOD IS –?'

And then he stopped mid-sentence and said:

'WHY HAVE YOU ALL GOT MOUS-TACHES ON YOUR FACES?'

He walked up and down the hallway, shouting:

'I WANT EVERY FIRST YEAR STUDENT IN THIS SCHOOL TO BE DRESSED AND IN THE ASSEMBLY HALL IN EXACTLY FIVE MINUTES' TIME!'

I looked at Conor and Barry. Uh oh!

Four minutes and fifty-nine seconds later, we were all in the assembly hall. Mr Cuffe got us to stand there in lines, with our arms by our sides, like soldiers in an inspection parade.

I was still hoping that, any minute now, he would start to see the funny side of it and say that whoever was responsible had given us all a great laugh and we should give them a round of applause for their efforts to cheer everyone up post-Christmas.

But he didn't say that. Instead, he walked up and

down the lines, staring into each of our faces, and he said:

'Last night, a boy – or boys – brought disgrace on this institute of learning by behaving like a hooligan. Or hooligans.'

Behind him, I could see Father Billings shaking his head in a disappointed way.

*PPPPPPHHHHHHFFFFFFAAAAAAR-RRRRRTTTTTT!!!!!!!*

For once, nobody laughed. No one wanted to draw attention to himself.

'I want to give the boy – or boys – responsible the opportunity to admit what he – or they – have done,' he said. 'If you were involved in putting graffiti on the faces of your fellow students, then raise your hand now!'

I was standing with Conor on one side of me and Barry on the other. Out of the corner of his mouth, Conor whispered, 'Don't raise your hands, fellas. If we don't own up, they'll never know it was us.'

I had no intention of raising my hand.

'Very well,' said Mr Cuffe. 'It's not going to take the world's greatest detective to solve this particular crime anyway.'

And that's when he said it:

'Would every boy in the assembly hall who *has* a

moustache drawn on his face please sit down on the floor?'

After a moment's pause, every boy in the assembly hall sat down on the floor – every boy, that is, except me and Conor!

I looked around. To my shock, I discovered that Barry had drawn a moustache on his own face to cover up his involvement in the crime!

Why didn't he tell *us* to do that?

Father Billings smiled at me and Conor in a sad way.

*PPPPPPHHHHHHFFFFFFAAAAAAR-RRRRRTTTTTT!!!!!!!*

'You two, come with me,' Mr Cuffe said. 'You are in big, BIG trouble!'

# 12 *The Right Place at the Right Time*

I sat in Mr Cuffe's office while he talked to Dad on the phone.

'Yes, Mr D'Arcy, he *does* have way too much energy!' he said. 'A Labrador with a big, red bow – oh, that's a good one, Mr D'Arcy! I should punish him in whatever way I consider appropriate, you say? Yes, you may rest assured that I will do that, Mr D'Arcy! Thank you so much!'

He put down the phone and smiled at me across the desk.

He had already given Conor his punishment – to pull up every single weed in the school grounds. Now, it was my turn.

'Mr Murray tells me you're rather keen on rugby,' he said.

Oh, no, I thought. Was he going to stop me from playing it? That would be the worst punishment EVER!

'Did you know,' he said, 'that the school team are playing today?'

'Yes, Mr Cuffe,' I said.

They were playing Blackrock College at three o'clock here in the school.

'I would like you to clean the dressing rooms,' he said, 'before the match . . .'

'Okay,' I replied.

That didn't seem so bad.

'. . . making sure that every surface is shining . . .'

'It will be.'

'. . . and I want you to use this!'

He handed me a toothbrush.

'A toothbrush?' I said. Was he mad? 'I can't clean an entire dressing room with a toothbrush! It'll take ages!'

'You'd better get started, then,' he said. 'There's only six hours until kick-off!'

I decided to just take it on the chin. I had to admit that what we'd done probably had *possibly* crossed a line. It turned out that the black markers we'd used to draw moustaches on all the other boys were

semi-permanent, which meant it would take weeks before they were all washed off.

I headed for the dressing rooms with the toothbrush and I set to work. I scrubbed the floor, then I scrubbed the walls, then I scrubbed the showers, then I scrubbed the sinks. And by half-past two — thirty minutes before kick-off — the room was as clean as an operating theatre.

I sat in the corner and admired my handiwork. And that was when the door suddenly flew open.

In they walked — the members of the school team. I felt very, very small in their presence, which was good, because I knew that I didn't belong there and I didn't want anyone to notice me.

Something was wrong with them, though. They didn't seem excited. They didn't seem up for the match at all. They appeared to be in no hurry to change out of their school uniforms and into their rugby gear.

Mr Murray was one of the last to enter the dressing room. He was talking to John Michael Ennis, who was the team's full-back and star player. The coach sounded concerned.

'Are you absolutely sure?' he asked him.

I noticed that John Michael had tears in his eyes.

'It happened when I stood up from my desk an hour ago,' he said. 'I felt my hamstring snap. There's no way I can play, Coach.'

Some of the other players started kicking the lockers and even the walls in anger and frustration.

'It's over!' they shouted. 'There's NO WAY we can win it without him!'

Mr Murray looked around the dressing room, at each player in turn.

'What kind of attitude is that?' he asked.

'We're playing Blackrock!' the team's captain, Midge Donnelly, said.

I'd heard that this Blackrock team was supposed to be one of the best teams in the history of schools rugby. They called them THE DREAM TEAM.

Mr Murray clapped his two hands together.

'Come on,' he said, 'let's try to come up with a solution to this.'

And then, suddenly, he was looking at me.

'What are you doing here?' he asked.

It was the first time anyone had noticed me sitting in the corner. And now EVERYONE was staring at me.

'I just came in to, er, clean the dressing room,' I said.

I saw a flash of something in his eyes.

'Can you play full-back for the school today?' he asked.

I watched everyone's jaws drop. I felt pretty much in shock myself.

'*Him?*' Midge said. 'Who is *he*?'

'His name is Gordon D'Arcy,' Mr Murray said. 'He's Ian D'Arcy's little brother.'

Midge just shook his head. 'I mean, how *old* is he?' he asked.

'Doesn't matter how old he is,' Mr Murray said. 'If he's good enough, he's old enough.'

'But *is* he good enough?' Midge said. 'That's the question.'

They all stared at me, sizing me up. I felt myself shrinking even further against the wall. Was I good enough? I didn't really think so. But if Mr Murray thought so . . .

'He's a really special player,' Mr Murray said. 'He has unbelievable skills and he reads the game brilliantly. The only question is whether or not he's ready to play at this level. I'm willing to take a chance on him.'

Mr Murray fixed me with a look then.

'So what do you say? Do you think you could do a job for us at full-back today?' he asked.

'I don't know,' I said. 'I've become kind of comfortable playing inside-centre.'

Everyone laughed. Which was kind of understandable.

'Gordon,' he said, 'you're being offered the opportunity to play for the school team in the Leinster Schools Senior Cup.'

Now that he put it like that . . .

'Okay,' I said. 'I'll play.'

# 13 *Dream Time*

We changed out of our school uniforms and into our rugby gear.

Midge threw me a jersey with the number fifteen on the back of it and I didn't hesitate. I pulled my school jumper over my head with the shirt still inside it, then dropped them on the dressing-room floor.

Next, I pulled on the jersey. The famous purple and white of Clongowes Wood College!

It was about five sizes too big for me. But I was so proud to wear it.

Mr Murray gave us our pre-match instructions.

'Don't think about the opposition,' he said. 'Forget all the things you've heard about them. It seems to me that every team these days is called a Dream Team. They haven't won anything yet, okay?'

'Okay,' we said.

'Just focus on your own game.'

Then he took me to one side for a quiet word.

'They're going to laugh at you when you walk out there,' he told me, 'and I want you to be ready for that. They're going to laugh at you because they think you're too young to play for the school. I just want to say to you that age is totally irrelevant. The only thing that matters is what's up here,' and he tapped the side of his head with his finger. Then he pointed at his heart. 'And in here,' he added. 'I've seen you play and I know you're capable of doing this. Now go out there and enjoy yourself.'

After hearing that, I felt like I could have walked through the dressing-room wall.

One or two of our players started shouting, 'Come on, Clongowes!' and the excitement took hold. Then out of the dressing room we walked, in single file, to face Blackrock College.

The atmosphere was electric. There were about a thousand people at the match – half of them Clongowes students, half of them Blackrock.

Mr Murray was right. As soon as the Blackrock supporters saw me, they fell around laughing. I suppose I *was* a strange sight. I was smaller than everyone else on the team and the number fifteen jersey was down to my knees.

I started to do my stretches and I could hear the comments that were being shouted in my direction:

'What are you, the Clongowes mascot or something?'

*That* got a huge laugh.

And: 'Do your mummy and daddy know you're here today?'

I tried to blank it out. But then I heard some familiar voices shouting my name. I turned around and I spotted Conor, Peter and Barry staring at me from the crowd, their mouths open.

'What the hell are you doing?' Conor shouted. He was laughing.

'I'm playing full-back,' I shouted back. 'John Michael Ennis is injured.'

'What? Seriously?'

But the person who was MOST surprised to see me on the field was Mr Cuffe. I watched him do a double-take when he spotted me doing my shuttle runs. The last time he'd set eyes on me was a few hours ago when he'd sent me to clean the dressing rooms with a toothbrush – and now I was about to lineout for the school!

He couldn't believe what he was seeing. He kept

closing his eyes, then opening them again, like he was convinced I was some kind of illusion that would go away.

The match kicked off.

I would be lying if I said the first ten minutes were the best ten minutes of rugby I ever played. I was nervous and I had the touch of a new-born giraffe.

I dropped the first high ball that came my way . . .

And a couple of times I knocked the ball on . . .

I heard the Blackrock supporters laughing. Someone shouted: 'Oh my God, that kid is WAY out of his depth!'

But then I could hear Conor and Peter shouting encouragement at me.

'You're doing great, Gordon!'

I also heard Barry say: 'Are you joking? He's making a complete show of himself!'

I could see why Blackrock were called the Dream Team. They ran circles around us. But they also beat us up. They were stronger than us. Whenever I jumped up in the air to make a catch, I was knocked to the ground . . .

And when I found myself at the bottom of a ruck, it felt like a herd of elephants had fallen on top of me . . .

But then, after fifteen minutes, I caught a high ball, tucked it under my arm and set off on a run, beating one player, then another, then another, before I was finally tackled.

And I could hear the laughter of the crowd suddenly go silent. It was like they were admiring this little kid's courage to have a go like that.

And then, as if by magic, everything suddenly clicked.

And I mean EVERYTHING!

I caught every ball that came my way. I slipped every tackle. I made passes I didn't think I was capable of making. And I made tackle after tackle.

And suddenly my teammates, including Midge, were slapping me on the back and saying, 'Well done! What's your name again?'

And I said, 'Gordon D'Arcy.'

And Midge said, 'Well done, Darce!' which was what they'd called Ian in his day. And now, apparently, it was my nickname as well.

Through some very stubborn defending, we managed to do something that no one had ever done against this Blackrock team – we stopped them scoring a try in the first half.

We went back to the dressing at half-time, only 9–6 behind.

The coach smiled at me. 'You're doing great,' he said. 'Just keep doing what you're doing.'

Then he addressed us as a team. 'Try to stop them getting any more points for as long as you can!' he said. 'Trust me, one of you is going to get a chance to score in the second half – and it'll probably be our *only* chance! When it happens, make sure you take it!'

Half-time went by in the blink of an eye. Suddenly, it was time to go back out again. I couldn't wait.

The atmosphere was even better in the second half. It was like the Blackrock crowd realized they'd come up against a team that was a match for them.

The Blackrock players increased the pressure, looking for the breakthrough try that would put distance between them and us. But we continued to keep them out – sometimes after they'd been camped on our line for a full five minutes.

And then, out of nowhere, I heard something that brought tears to my eyes. Our supporters had started singing. They were singing *that* song:

> *Mill 'em, Darce!*
> *Na na na!*
> *Mill 'em, Darce!*
> *Na na na!*

*You better hope and pray*
*You don't get in his way,*
*Mill 'em, Darce!*
*Na na na!*

Except they weren't singing it about Ian. Now, they were singing it about me!

I suddenly felt about twelve inches taller – in other words, the same size as everyone else!

Every time I made a tackle, there was a roar from the crowd – even from the Blackrock fans, who couldn't believe what they were seeing.

We held back wave after wave of attacks. And it was exhausting. But we managed to keep the score at 9–6 until ten minutes from the end. Then one of their centres, David Quinlan, was running with the ball. And for no apparent reason, he tripped over . . .

And the ball spilled out of his hands . . .

And fell right at my feet . . .

And I remembered what the coach said: 'One of you is going to get a chance – and it'll probably be our *only* chance.'

And I thought to myself, This is it. This *is* that chance. And it's fallen to ME!

So I bent down and I scooped the ball up in my hands. And from that moment, everything . . .

. . . seemed to go . . .

. . . into slow . . .

. . . motion . . .

I was aware that I had the ball under my arm and I was running . . .

I was aware that there was half a rugby pitch between me and the line . . .

I could hear the roars of the crowd, but the sound was muffled, like they were far away, in the distance . . .

And over that, I could hear the sound of my breathing . . .

And my heart pounding . . .

And my feet hitting the hard ground . . .

And behind me I could hear the sound of Blackrock players gaining on me fast . . .

Like a stampede of horses . . .

And then someone threw his arms around my legs . . .

I could feel them closing around me . . .

And I could feel myself falling . . .

The ground rose up to hit my face . . .

Like when I fell from the top bunk . . .

And then I heard Conor and Peter yelling, 'Ground the ball! *Ground the ball!*'

And I realized that I still had it in my hands . . .

And the line was just in front of me . . .

An arm's length away . . .

I stretched out with the ball in my hand . . .

And I planted it . . .

Right on the line!

The roar of our supporters was deafening. I was helped to my feet and I looked over at Conor and Peter. They were jumping around with excitement.

We were in front! It was 11–9! We were beating Blackrock – the so-called Dream Team!

We scored the conversion. But we knew we still had work to do. Eight minutes to the whistle and a squad of seriously angry Blackrock players to deal with.

Blackrock came back at us. It was attack after attack and it seemed certain that they were going to score. But we defended . . .

And defended . . .

And defended . . .

And then, with the time almost up, Blackrock's outhalf, Emmet Farrell, got the ball in his hands. He beat one player . . .

Then another . . .

Then another . . .

Until I was the only man standing between him and a certain try under the posts.

He tried to sell me a dummy. He pretended to go one way, then he went the other. But I readjusted my body. And then . . .

BANG!

I tackled him low . . .

I picked him up . . .

And I drove him backwards . . .

The ball spilled loose. I kicked it out of play. The referee blew the whistle.

It was over!

We had done something that everyone except Mr Murray thought impossible!

We had beaten Blackrock!

Our supporters spilled onto the field. I felt myself being lifted up. I looked down and discovered that I was sitting on Flash Barry's shoulders.

'You did it, Gordon!' he shouted. 'I knew you would!'

# 14  *A Surprise Visitor*

Things changed for me after that. It all happened very quickly. People forgot that I was the kid who drew moustaches on the faces of my fellow First Year students. Suddenly, I was the boy who scored the try that beat the Blackrock Dream Team!

It was an odd feeling. Everyone in the school suddenly knew my name – even boys I'd never met before.

Everywhere I went it was, 'Hey, Gordon!' and 'You the man, Darce!'

Now, as well as training with the First Years during Free Time, I was training with the Senior Cup team every lunchtime, too.

One afternoon, a couple of weeks after the Blackrock match, I was sitting in English class. We were studying *Romeo and Juliet* by William Shakespeare.

Mr Curran, the teacher, was asking if any of us knew what one character was saying to another.

I had no idea. It was all 'ye' this and 'wherefore art' that. I couldn't understand why they couldn't just speak plain English. I was bored. I was looking out the window when I noticed a crowd of people playing rugby on the pitch outside.

I made an excuse to get out of class. I told Mr Curran that I desperately needed the toilet, then I slipped outside.

As I got closer to the pitch, I realized that the players were all girls.

They were REALLY good.

But one girl was better than all the others. She zigzagged her way around the field, beating player after player . . .

She pinged around the most brilliant passes . . .

And she tackled the other girls with UN-BELIEVABLE ferocity . . .

It was Conor's cousin, Aoife.

When they were finished, I gave her a wave and she came over to me.

'So Bridget's have a team now?' I asked.

'Yeah,' she said, 'this was our first training session. Mr Cuffe has given us permission to use your pitch.'

'You're actually REALLY good!'

'So you don't think it's just a man's game any-more, then?'

I turned red with embarrassment.

'No,' I said, 'not anymore.'

'Did it hurt,' she asked, 'when I tackled you like that?'

I laughed.

'It was more my pride than anything,' I told her.

'I heard you played really well against Blackrock,' she said.

'Oh, em, thanks. Hey, maybe me and you could train together sometime?'

'I'd love that,' she said. Then she smiled. 'Maybe I could teach you one or two things!'

I had to amire her. She was very much her own person.

Just then, I heard a voice behind me shout: 'Mii-isteeerrr D'Aaarrrrcccyyy!'

I froze. It was Mr Murray. When teachers referred to you as 'Mister', it was usually because you were in some kind of trouble.

I turned around. I was trying to think of an excuse to explain why I wasn't in English class, but I couldn't think of anything. I opened my mouth and all that came out was:

'I . . . Em . . . Em . . . Er . . .'

But Mr Murray didn't seem at all bothered that I was standing outside talking to a girl when I should have been inside learning about *Romeo and Juliet*.

'You have a visitor,' he said. 'He's with Mr Cuffe and Father Billings right now.'

A visitor? That was odd.

We started walking towards the school.

'Who is it?' I asked.

'Look, *he'll* explain everything to you,' the coach replied. 'But what I *would* like to say to you is that, well, you're about to be offered a wonderful opportunity. The kind of opportunity that most kids your age can only dream of. You'll look back on it one day and you'll say it was either the BEST thing that ever happened to you or the WORST thing that ever happened to you. And which one it is, Gordon, is entirely up to you.'

I had literally no idea what he was talking about.

We reached Mr Cuffe's office. Mr Murray knocked on the door three times. I heard Mr Cuffe shout:

'COME IN!'

And into the office we went. I looked around. Mr Cuffe was sitting behind his desk and Father Billings was standing behind him. And now *I* was the one who was forced to do a double-take. Because on the opposite side of the desk was a man I had only ever seen on TV before.

It was Warren Gatland, the coach of the Ireland rugby team!

He stood up and extended his hand to me.

'Gordon?' he said. 'I'm Warren.'

'Yeah, I know!' I replied.

I was in shock.

'How are you going?' he asked.

He spoke with an accent that sounded unusual to me. That was because he was from New Zealand, the country where the All Blacks came from.

'I'm . . . I'm . . . fine,' I said, more than a little star-struck.

Why did Warren Gatland want to meet me? That's all I could think.

'I saw you play,' he said, 'against Blackrock. You really impressed me.'

But it was what he said next that shocked me. I mean, it REALLY rocked me back on my heels.

He said: 'How would you like to train with the Ireland squad?'

## 15 'Okay, Dad, Brace Yourself!'

Mr Cuffe allowed me a moment alone in the office to ring Dad and tell him what had happened. I didn't want him to just switch on the TV news and see his son flinging the ball around with the Ireland rugby team. The shock might kill him stone dead!

So I picked up the phone receiver and I dialled his work number. He answered after four rings.

'Bank of Ireland, Wexford,' he said in a sing-song voice. 'How may I help you?'

'Dad?' I said.

'Gordon,' he replied, 'what's wrong? Is everything okay?'

'Okay, Dad, brace yourself!' I said excitedly. 'You are not going to BELIEVE what I'm about to tell you!'

'Wait a minute,' he said, 'where are you phoning from?'

'I'm phoning from Mr Cuffe's office,' I told him.

'I might have known! Right, what have you done now?'

'I haven't done anything, Dad.'

'You drew *beards* on everyone's faces this time, didn't you? Or was it glasses?'

'Dad, will you please stop talking for just ten seconds! I'm not in trouble.'

'Not in trouble? Then why on Earth are you back in Mr Cuffe's office – again?'

'Warren Gatland wanted to see me.'

'Warren Gatland? I'm afraid you've lost me, Gordon. The only Warren Gatland I know is the one who coaches the Ireland rugby team!'

'Yeah, that's the one I'm talking about, Dad!'

'But why in the name of God would Warren Gatland want to see you? Please tell me you didn't draw a beard and glasses on Warren Gatland?'

'Dad, will you forget about the whole drawing on people's faces thing? That was a one-off and I've already apologized for it. Look, are you sitting down?'

'Of course I'm sitting down! I work in a bank!'

'Okay, then I'll tell you my news! Here goes! Warren Gatland . . . has invited me . . . to train with the Ireland rugby squad!'

'To train?'

'Yes.'

'With the Ireland rugby squad?'

'Yes.'

'Is this some kind of joke, Gordon?'

'It's not a joke, Dad! It turns out he saw me play for the school against Blackrock a few weeks ago! He thought I played really well!'

'You did play really well! I read it in the newspaper! You scored the try that beat the so-called Dream Team!'

'There you are, then!'

'And he thinks you're ready, does he? To play for Ireland?'

'I'm not *playing* for Ireland! I'm training *with* Ireland! There's a big difference.'

'Right.'

'He just liked a couple of things I did on the pitch and he thinks I might be one for the future.'

'So it's just to give you some experience?'

'I suppose that's it, yeah.'

'It's still a big honour, Gordon!'

'I know.'

'A huge honour. I mean, think of the players you're going to be training with. Brian O'Driscoll! Peter Stringer! And of course there's Ronan O'Gara!'

'Okay, Dad, will you please stop naming names? I'm nervous enough as it is!'

'Sorry, Gordon, it's just a bit hard to get my head around it. So when is it happening?' he asked. 'This training session, I mean?'

'Tomorrow afternoon,' I told him. 'They're training in Greystones, County Wicklow.'

'Right!' he said. 'I'm taking the day off!'

'What? Seriously?'

'My son has been invited to train with the Ireland rugby team! You don't think I'm going to miss *that*, do you?'

'That's good, because I'm going to need a lift!'

I could hear that he was excited.

'I'll drive up in the morning,' he said, 'pick you up from school, then we'll head for – where did you say, Greystones?'

'Greystones,' I said. 'That's right.'

'This is a very exciting thing, Gordon. It's the opportunity of a lifetime.'

'I know.'

'I'll see you tomorrow! And try not to draw anything on anyone's face in the meantime, okay?'

Conor couldn't believe the news when I told him later that day. Even Peter looked up from his chemistry book and said:

'WHAT? You can't be serious! You *are* serious? No!'

I laughed.

'I know,' I said. 'I can hardly believe it myself.'

It was Free Time and we were hanging around in our dorm room. I was packing my kit bag.

'That's, like, mind-blowing!' Conor said. 'That is the most amazing thing I've ever heard in my entire life!'

'It's brilliant for you,' Peter said. 'And you earned it.'

It was nice that my friends were so pleased for me. Then Barry walked in.

'Earned what?' he asked.

No one answered him. To be honest, none of us knew whether to trust him anymore after he managed to worm his way out of the moustache incident.

'Come on,' he said, 'you can tell me.'

'Gordon has been invited to train with the Ireland rugby squad,' Conor said.

'WHAT? The ACTUAL Ireland rugby squad?'

'Yeah,' said Peter. 'It turns out that Warren Gatland saw him play against Blackrock and thinks he has a lot of potential.'

Barry shook his head.

'I can't believe,' he said, 'that an actual friend of mine is going to be training with the Ireland rugby squad. And don't worry, Darce, you don't have to thank me!'

'What?' I said. 'Why would I thank *you*?'

'Hey, it wouldn't have happened if it wasn't for me, would it?'

'How do you figure that out?'

'Well, think about it. If I hadn't drawn a moustache on my own face, *I* might have been sent to clean those dressing rooms instead of you. And you never would have been picked to play for the school team. And you never would have scored that try against Blackrock. And Warren Gatland never would have seen you play.'

He had a point, I suppose.

'But like I said,' he added, 'you don't have to thank me.'

Conor couldn't take the smile off his face.

'Gordon,' he said, 'this is the best thing that's ever happened to ANY of us! Are you nervous?'

'Terrified,' I admitted. 'Brian O'Driscoll. Paul O'Connell. Ronan O'Gara. I'm definitely not in their league.'

'Don't think like that, Gordon!' Conor said. 'Warren Gatland wouldn't be inviting you to train with them if he didn't think you were good enough!'

'Do you think?'

'Trust me! You're going to do great! And it's only training, bear in mind. It's not like he's asking you to lineout against France!'

# 16  *A Special Guest*

Dad collected me from school the following day. I think he was more nervous than I was because he talked nonstop for the entire hour it took to drive from Clongowes Wood College to Greystones Rugby Club.

'Do you know what I was thinking about,' he said, 'while I was driving up from Wexford this morning?'

'What?' I asked.

'I was thinking about the first time we ever watched rugby together – do you remember that?'

'Of course I remember it! Simon Geoghegan!'

'Simon Geoghegan! The very man! You wanted to be just like him! And now look at you!'

'You're not going to cry, Dad, are you?'

'I might very well cry! But sure, what if I do? I

mean, it seems like only yesterday that I brought you down to Jimmy O'Connor at Wexford Wanderers – and now you're training with the –'

His voice cracked.

'Dad!' I said.

'I'm sorry,' he said. 'I promised your mother I'd try to hold it together at least until I drop you back to Clongowes tonight. Then I'll probably cry the whole way back down the N11.'

We reached Greystones Rugby Club and we got out of the car.

I could see that the players were out on the pitch, warming up. I was already wearing my rugby gear – not my Clongowes jersey, but the one I used to wear when I played for Wexford Wanderers. It was partly out of pride for the club and the town that made me – and partly because I promised Jimmy O'Connor that if I ever got to train with Ireland, I would wear my club colours.

Dad stood on the sideline and I joined the others. While I performed my stretching exercises, I became aware that the rest of the team were looking at me. But I was too scared to look back at them.

Then I heard a voice say, 'Gordon, is it?'

I looked up. It was Paul O'Connell.

It was THE Paul O'Connell!

The ACTUAL Paul O'Connell!

'I'm Paul O'Connell,' he said, offering me his hand. So I shook it. He told me I was very welcome to the session and he started to introduce me to the rest of the players.

'This is Ronan O'Gara. This is Brian O'Driscoll. This is Peter Stringer. This is Rob Kearney.'

I had to fight back the urge to shout: 'I KNOW WHO YOU ALL ARE! I'VE SEEN YOU ON TV!'

Instead, I shook their hands in turn and I said, 'It's nice to meet you. I'm Gordon. Although some people call me Darce.'

'What's the jersey?' Ronan O'Gara asked me.

'It's, er, Wexford Wanderers,' I said.

He pulled a face.

'Is that where you're from?' he asked.

'Yeah,' I said. 'Wexford Town.'

'Well,' he said with a grin, 'we all have our crosses to bear, don't we? You're exactly what we need around here, though – another Leinster lad!'

'Don't listen to ROG,' Paul O'Connell said. 'So you're training with us today, huh?'

'Yeah,' I said, 'Warren Gatland invited me.'

'I saw what you did against Blackrock College,' Brian O'Driscoll said.

'Oh, er, thanks,' I replied.

'Hey, I didn't say I liked it,' he said. 'I *went* to Blackrock College.'

'Oh, er, sorry.'

He laughed then.

'You played great,' he said. 'And it's good to have you training with us today.'

A second or two later, Warren Gatland walked across the pitch.

'Ah,' he said, 'I see you've all met our guest. Now, I know he's new to the set-up, but I don't want any of you to go easy on him. He's here to learn.'

As we started training, I still felt like I was in

a dream. Looking around me at all the famous faces, I had to keep reminding myself to close my mouth.

Everyone was nice to me – but they definitely *didn't* go easy on me. Once, Brian O'Driscoll threw a pass and I fumbled it.

'Darce!' he yelled at me. 'Focus! Come on, we're not doing this for fun!'

A few minutes later, Ronan O'Gara tackled me hard and dumped me on my back and I lost the ball in the process.

He held out his hand and helped me up off the ground. As he did so he whispered to me, 'You're doing well – keep it up.'

I began to feel less in awe of the other players as the session wore on. I started to see them not as stars but as ordinary lads who just happened to be great at rugby.

Soon, I was calling them by their nicknames. Not Ronan O'Gara, but ROG. Not Peter Stringer, but Strings. Not Brian O'Driscoll, but BOD. Not Paul O'Connell, but Paulie.

And I trained harder than I'd ever trained before. By the time it was finished, I felt exhausted.

'Well done!' Warren Gatland told me. 'You did great out there!'

Dad decided to embarrass me then.

'So do you think he's got something, Warren?' he asked. 'Did you see any little flashes?'

Warren laughed.

'Yeah,' he said, 'your son is a terrific young talent.'

'One for the future, Warren?' Dad asked.

Warren shook his head.

'No,' he replied.

I was so disappointed.

'Look,' he added, 'I don't know if you know this, but we've got this game against France in Paris in three days' time.'

'I know,' I said. 'I'm going home to Wexford for the weekend. Me and Dad are going to watch it on TV.'

'What if I told you that you didn't have to watch it on TV?'

I thought he was about to offer me and Dad free tickets to the match. But it turned out to be something bigger than that.

Much bigger.

He looked at Dad and he said, 'I've spoken to the school and they're good with it as long as it doesn't interfere with his schoolwork.'

'Good with what?' Dad asked.

And Warren said, 'We'd like Gordon to come to Paris as part of the Ireland squad.'

At that point, Dad burst into tears.

Warren smiled and said, 'I'll take that as a yes, then!'

## 17 Something Big. Something Very, VERY Big

Dad *did* cry – all the way back to Clongowes, in fact. But then I couldn't blame him because I felt SERIOUSLY teary myself. You have to understand, my world had suddenly changed completely. And it had happened in the course of just a few weeks. My head was spinning trying to keep up with it all.

'I want you to know,' Dad said, 'that I'm so proud of you, Gordon.'

'Thanks, Dad!' I replied. 'Maybe keep your eyes on the road, though!'

'You should ring your mother and tell her the news. Use my phone there.'

I picked up Dad's mobile and I phoned the house in Wexford.

Mum answered. 'Hello?' she said.

'Hey, Mum,' I said, 'it's me!'

'How did you get on, Love?'

'Not great,' I said, winking at Dad. 'I'm starting to think that maybe rugby isn't the game for me after all.'

'Oh, Gordon,' she said in a soothing voice. 'I meant to tell your Dad to warn you not to get your hopes up. I know how carried away you can get.'

'Oh, well, it was a nice dream while it lasted.'

'It was a good experience for you to have, Gordon. Even if it came to nothing. There's not many boys your age can say they trained with the Ireland rugby team.'

I couldn't keep the news to myself any longer.

'Mum,' I said, 'I'm in the squad for the game against France!'

'What?' she asked.

'Warren Gatland has included me in the squad. I'm going to Paris with the team tomorrow.'

There was silence on the other end of the phone. Then I heard a bump.

'Hello?' I said. 'HELLO?'

'What's going on?' Dad asked.

'I don't know,' I said. 'She isn't saying anything. HELLO?'

A second or two later, I heard Shona's voice on the line.

'What did you say to her?' she asked.

'I just told her that Warren Gatland had put me in the Ireland squad for the Six Nations opener in Paris this weekend.'

'She's after fainting, Gordon!'

'Oh, God. I'm sorry.'

I looked at Dad. 'She fainted,' I told him.

'You shouldn't be playing tricks on her like that,' Shona said.

'It's not a trick,' I tried to tell her. 'It's the truth.'

'Truth, my eye! That's it, Mum! You're okay! I'm just going to make you a nice mug of sugary tea!'

The line went dead.

'Is your mother okay?' Dad asked.

'Yeah,' I said, 'Shona's making her tea. She didn't believe me, by the way. She thought I was making it up.'

Dad laughed.

'It's a lot to take in,' he said. 'I'm not even sure *I* believe it yet.'

Eventually, we arrived back at Clongowes Wood.

'Don't forget to phone us in the morning before you leave for Paris,' Dad reminded me.

I said I would.

'And phone us when you arrive as well,' he said.

I said I would.

'And remember, Gordon,' he said, 'just keep the head, okay?'

He gave me a hug, then he drove off.

As I was walking into the school, I spotted Aoife, alone on the rugby field, practising her kicking. She was taking shots at goal from different angles and distances – all of them difficult.

She worked so hard on her game. She really was an inspiration.

She was sizing up a kick near to the touchline when I walked over to her.

'Hey, Aoife,' I said.

But she didn't answer me. Such was her concentration, she didn't seem to see or hear me. She took the kick and the ball sailed straight between the two posts. Only then did she spot me standing there.

'Oh, I'm sorry,' she said. 'I was in another world. So how did it go?'

'Go?' I asked.

'Conor said you were invited to train with the Ireland team.'

'Oh, yeah, it was, em, good fun.'

I was bursting to tell her the big news. But Warren had asked me to keep it within the family – at least until he made the official announcement tomorrow morning.

'Will you do me a favour?' she asked.

'Sure,' I said, 'what is it?'

'Will you go and get that ball for me?'

She meant the one she'd just kicked that was FIFTY metres away.

And there I was, an almost-Ireland rugby international, being asked to retrieve balls for her. I didn't complain, though. I went and got the ball, then I handed it to her. She bent down, placed it in the kicking tee, then measured out three steps backwards and four to the left.

'So what's Ronan O'Gara like?' she wanted to know.

'He's nice,' I said. 'He's got a kind of weird sense of humour. You have to get used to it.'

'Because he's my absolute hero. And what's Brian O'Driscoll like?'

'Sound. The surprising thing is, Aoife, when you actually meet them, they're no different to anyone else. Anyway, I'll leave you to it.'

She didn't answer me. She was focusing hard on the posts again.

I walked into the school, where I ran into Father Billings in the lobby.

'AH, THE VERY MAN!' he said, loud enough to wake the whole of Europe. 'I SPOKE TO THAT NICE MR GATLAND ON THE PHONE AND I TOLD HIM THAT THE SCHOOL HAS NO OBJECTION TO YOU GOING TO PARIS – PROVIDED IT DOESN'T HAVE A NEGATIVE IMPACT ON YOUR SCHOOLWORK, OF COURSE! IT'S OBVIOUSLY A BIG HONOUR FOR YOU – BUT IT'S ALSO A BIG HONOUR FOR CLONGOWES WOOD COLLEGE, TOO!'

I looked around. The lobby was full of boys, who could all hear what he was saying.

'Father Billings,' I said in a hushed tone, 'I've been asked to keep it quiet until they announce the squad tomorrow morning.'

But he couldn't hear me.

'IT'S NOT EVERY SCHOOL IN THE COUNTRY THAT CAN BOAST THAT ONE OF ITS PUPILS HAS BEEN CALLED INTO THE IRELAND RUGBY SQUAD!'

I heard a murmur of interest among the other boys.

'Did he just say that Darce is in the Ireland squad?'

'AND PARIS!' Father Billings continued. 'WHAT A WONDERFUL CITY! HAVE YOU BEEN THERE BEFORE?'

'No, Father,' I said. 'I've never been on an air-plane before. Maybe we could have this conversation somewhere else, where there aren't loads of people listening?'

'WELL, BEST OF LUCK WITH IT! *IF* YOU GET ON THE FIELD, THAT IS. YOU MIGHT BE JUST A SUB, OF COURSE! EITHER WAY, WE'LL ALL BE CHEERING YOU ON!'

I watched the other kids scuttle off to spread the news.

'BY THE WAY,' Father Billings said, 'MR GATLAND SAID HE WANTED TO KEEP THE WHOLE THING QUIET UNTIL TOMORROW MORNING, SO TRY TO KEEP THE NEWS TO YOURSELF FOR NOW! MUM'S THE WORD, EH?'

He broke wind.

*PHHHFFFAAARRRTTT!!!*

Then he walked off.

By the time I got back to my room, the news was all over the school. Conor and Peter were standing there with their eyes and mouths wide open, having just heard it.

'You're IN the Ireland team for Paris?' Conor said.

He sounded delighted for me.

'The squad,' I said. 'He hasn't picked the team yet.'

'That's amazing news!'

'You know if you play,' Peter said, 'you'll be the first Wexford Wanderer EVER to represent Ireland?'

I hadn't thought about that.

Barry was lying on the top bunk. He sat up.

'Can I be your agent?' he asked.

'Agent?' I said. 'I don't need an agent!'

'Of course you need an agent!' he said. 'When this news gets out, your name is going to be HUGE! Everyone is going to want a piece of Gordon D'Arcy! You're going to need someone to represent you!'

'What I need,' I said, 'is a good rest. A car is coming to collect me at five o'clock in the morning.'

# 18  *Paris, Here We Come!*

I was telling the truth when I said I'd never been on an airplane before. I hadn't. I'd been on plenty of buses. And I'd been on trains loads of times. But as for flying – well, it had never really come up.

Wexford didn't even have an airport.

But I still tried to act like it wasn't a big deal as I boarded the flight to Paris with the rest of the team.

I found the seat number on my ticket and I sat down next to the window. I looked out at all the other planes getting ready to take people all over the world.

A second or two later, BOD sat down beside me.

'So have you ever flown before?' he asked.

'Flown?' I said. 'Me? Oh, many times. Many, many times.'

I knew I was trying too hard to sound cool, but I couldn't help it.

'Great,' he said. 'So what countries have you been to?'

'Er, I'd have to check my passport to give you the full list,' I said. 'Can I come back to you later on that one?'

BOD laughed.

'Darce,' he said, 'I'm just making conversation here.'

'Right,' I said.

I probably needed to lighten up a bit.

I heard a loud rumble, the plane started to tremble and the pilot announced that we would soon be in the air. The plane tore down the runway. I felt this strange lightness in my chest, then I looked down to see Dublin disappearing below us.

I was very excited, but I tried my best to keep a lid on it during the ninety minutes we were in the air. Most of the players, including BOD, were quiet. Some were already thinking about the match, wondering whether they'd be in the team.

I suppose I was less worried because I was sure I wasn't going to be starting. They were the ones under pressure, not me.

I thought to myself how I'd usually be in Double Maths right now. Even if I ended up sitting on the bench for the entire match, at least I'd missed Double Maths!

An air hostess arrived with a trolley. She said, 'Can I get you a drink, Sir?'

Did she just call me Sir? In my world, Sir was something you called your teachers!

I tapped my pockets. 'Er, I actually don't have any –'

'You don't need money,' she said. 'It's free, Sir.'

'Free? In that case, I'll have a Coke, please. No, a Fanta. No, a 7-Up. No, maybe a Coke after all.'

BOD turned to me then. 'Darce,' he said, 'why don't you just get one of each?'

'One of each?' I asked. 'Is that allowed?'

'Absolutely,' the air hostess said, then she looked at BOD. 'And what about you, Sir?'

'Do you have any energy drinks?' he asked.

'No, I'm afraid not.'

'I'll just have water, then,' he said. 'I need to stay hydrated. We've got a big game tomorrow.'

'Actually,' I said, 'forget what I said about Coke and Fanta and 7-Up. I'll have water as well, please.'

Fizzy drinks made me burpy, I remembered. I didn't want to be belching my way through the national anthem tomorrow – even if I was just on the bench.

'I've seen you play for Leinster,' I told BOD. 'Loads of times.'

'Do you ever go to the matches?' he asked.

'Sometimes,' I said, 'with my dad. It was always my ambition to play for Leinster one day.'

'Not for Ireland?'

'Yeah, for Ireland as well, obviously.'

'Maybe I'll tell ROG that you were more excited about playing for Leinster than playing for Ireland!'

'Okay, PLEASE don't do that!'

'I'm joking, Darce!'

'Oh, right!'

We landed in Paris, then we boarded a bus to take us into the city. We had a police escort to accompany us to the team hotel. We drove through the streets with two French policemen riding on motorbikes in front of the bus, and two behind, all with their sirens blaring.

I stared out the window and I took in all the sights.

'Look at that river!' I shouted. 'It's green!'

'That's the Seine,' ROG said.

'Why is it that colour? Did they dye it because they knew we were coming?'

ROG looked at me like I was mad. 'No,' he said, 'it's always that colour!'

'Look at that!' I said then, unable to contain my excitement as I spotted a huge archway.

In the seat behind me, Leo Cullen laughed. 'That's the Arc de Triomphe,' he said.

'The what?' I asked.

'Are you saying you've never seen the Arc de Triomphe before?'

A few months ago, the furthest I'd ever travelled was Gorey. But I didn't say that.

As we drove along the narrow, cobbled streets and the broad boulevards of Paris, people heard the sirens blaring and then spotted our bus, decked out in green, white and orange colours. They shook their fists at us and shouted, '*Allez, la France! Allez, la France!*'

'They seem very angry,' I said.

'They're just reminding you to reset your watch,' Conor Murray told me.

'Are they? Why?'

'Because Paris is six hours ahead of Ireland.'

'Is it?'

He laughed. 'I'm only winding you up,' he said.

'They do seem pretty angry, though,' I said.

'Wait till you experience the atmosphere in the Stade de France,' said Rob Kearney. 'You won't have felt anything like it before.'

'I don't know,' I said, 'it was always pretty intense whenever Wexford Wanderers played the Gorey Gladiators.'

Again, everyone seemed to find this amusing.

'It'll be even scarier than Wexford Wanderers against the Gorey Gladiators,' Conor Murray assured me.

As we got nearer to the hotel, Warren Gatland walked down the centre aisle of the bus and sat down next to me.

'How are you doing?' he said to me. 'You alright?'

'Yeah, fine,' I said. 'I didn't have the Coke or the Fanta or the 7-Up in the end. I just had water. I want to stay hydrated, obviously.'

'That's good,' he said. 'Because you're starting tomorrow.'

I couldn't believe what I was hearing. The shock must have told on my face.

'Don't look so surprised,' he said. 'I didn't drag you out of school so you could sit on the sidelines.'

'You're saying I'm in the actual team?' I asked. 'I'm going to be playing for *actual* Ireland?'

Warren laughed.

'Yes,' he said, 'you're going to be playing for *actual* Ireland. I want you to start at twelve. You're playing in the centre with Brian there.'

BOD gave me a nod across the aisle.

'Er, okay,' I said, trying not to let my voice shake and show how scared I was!

'I don't want to frighten you,' Warren said, 'but I realize that this is a lot of responsibility I'm heaping on your shoulders. Playing for your country is a lot of pressure at any age. But I saw you play for Clongowes against Blackrock. And I really do believe you're good enough to play at this level.'

I looked out the window and watched the streets of Paris zip by. And all I could think was that tomorrow was going to be the biggest day of my life.

# 19 *Putting the Fear of God in Them*

I didn't feel well. As a matter of fact, I felt positively *unwell*. It came on me very suddenly. My stomach was sick. My head felt light. My legs felt weak and hollow.

It was the day of the match. I was sitting in the dressing room in the Stade de France and the kick-off was less than an hour away.

All of the players were doing their own thing. Some were listening to music on their headphones. Some were stretching. Some were bandaging parts of their bodies that were sore. Others were sitting in silence, with their eyes closed, thinking about the match to come.

Conor O'Shea, the Ireland full-back, walked into the dressing room. I noticed that he was carrying something flat in his hands.

'Darce,' he said, 'this is something we do for every player before he plays for Ireland for the first time.'

I noticed that it was an Ireland jersey. It turned out to be *my* Ireland jersey.

'You only get to make your debut for your country once,' he said. 'And it's a very special moment – and it's important to mark that. So welcome to the squad, Darce.'

All of the other players clapped as he handed the

jersey to me. I spread it out across my lap and stared at it. I looked at the crest with the shamrock and the rugby ball on it and I touched it. This was really Ireland!

It was much heavier than I expected. The fabric was very thick, much thicker than my Wanderers and Clowgowes jerseys. I turned it over. On the back was the number twelve, then above it, across the shoulders, in white letters, it said, D'ARCY.

When I saw it, I got a lump in my throat.

I pulled the jersey over my head. It was HUGE on me. It stretched down to my knees. But that didn't matter because I just tucked it into my shorts, like I did the day I played against Blackrock. Then I caught sight of myself in the mirror and I felt a sudden surge of pride.

Warren gave us our instructions for the match. Then Paulie started shouting out lines to motivate us:

'LET'S PUT THE FEAR OF GOD INTO THEM! LET'S PUT THE FEAR OF GOD INTO THEM!'

Shortly afterwards, we were standing in the tunnel, waiting to walk out onto the pitch.

Conor Murray was standing behind me.

'Darce,' he said, 'you've got to breathe out.'

That's when I realized that I'd been holding my breath since we'd arrived at the stadium. That may have accounted for the light-headedness I was feeling in the dressing room. So I let the air out of my lungs.

ROG was standing in front of me. He turned around and smiled at me.

'Well, boy?' he said.

That was how Cork people said hello, I'd discovered.

'Just remember,' he said, 'it's a match like any other. Except there's a hundred thousand people out there and another hundred million watching on television!'

Okay, was that supposed to make me feel *less* nervous?

'Don't mind him. He's only winding you up,' BOD said.

The French players emerged from their dressing room and lined up beside us. Most of them I knew to see from TV. Serge Betson. Imanol Harinordoquy. Dmitri Yachvili.

Except they looked even BIGGER than they did on TV. Bigger and more fearsome.

Fabien Pelous looked like a monster with his enormous forehead and shoulders. All the French players had huge muscles and stubble and angry faces.

I watched them as they walked past me, then they stopped next to us and waited for the referee to tell us it was time to walk out onto the pitch.

I turned my head and I saw Mathieu Bastareaud standing next to me – the man I would be marking today. I had to do a double-take. He was built like the boiler house in Clongowes. He caught me staring at him and he laughed out loud.

'*Oh la la!*' he said, pointing at me. '*Il est si petit!*'[1]

All of the other French players turned to look at me and they laughed, too.

'*Il est plus petit que Peter Stringer!*'[2]

'Does anyone know what they're saying?' I asked. 'It's just, I don't speak French.'

ROG turned around to me again.

'Bastareaud's terrified of you!' he said out of the corner of his mouth. 'He was saying to the others, "Please, don't let him hurt me!"'

I had to admit, Bastareaud didn't *look* that terrified of me. As a matter of fact, he reached out his hand and tousled my hair.

'*Je vais te mettre dans ma poche,*' he said, '*petit garçon!*'[3]

---

[1] 'Wow! He is so small!'
[2] 'He is even smaller than Peter Stringer!'
[3] 'I'm going to put you in my pocket, little boy!'

Perhaps he was wishing me good luck, I thought. 'Thank you!' I replied. 'You, too.'

A few seconds later, we were given the signal to walk out. Paulie told me to brace myself for the noise.

'It's going to hit you like a baseball bat,' he warned me.

And he was right. It was deafening – to the point where I couldn't hear a word of what anyone was saying.

Strings was offering me some advice. I could see his lips moving, but I couldn't hear anything over the roar of the French crowd.

The stadium was huge. I looked up at the stands full of people and I wondered how could they even *see* the pitch from way up there?

We stood in a line and waited for the national anthems to begin. First, it was 'Ireland's Call'. We all sang along. But none of us could hear the music so we all had to guess where we were in the song. Some of us were a line or two ahead. Some of us were a line or two behind.

Next, it was the French national anthem, which is called 'La Marseillaise'. There was a respectful hush before it started. Thousands of people going:

'Ssshhh!!! Ssshhh!!! Ssshhh!!! Ssshhh!!! Ssshhh!!! Ssshhh!!!'

Then the brass band started to play and the entire stadium burst into song.

Something very strange happened then. A big cockerel walked past me. It turned out he was the French mascot. He walked the entire length of the Irish line as if he was inspecting us. It made me think of Princess Layer and how much my life had changed since I spent that summer on Uncle Tim and Auntie Kathleen's farm.

Then the anthems were finished and we all got into our positions. I looked at BOD.

'So, any advice?' I asked him.

'Yeah, it's very simple,' he said. 'Anywhere I go, you follow me. And anywhere you go, I follow you. Whenever Bastareaud gets the ball, one of us hits him hard to knock him off balance, then the other one knocks him down and lies on top of him.'

It sounded like a good plan to me. I mean, Bastareaud was so ENORMOUS, it was definitely going to take two of us to bring him down.

The referee blew his whistle. ROG kicked the ball high and deep into the French half, then Clément Poitrenaud caught it and kicked it right back into our half.

I knew from the instant it left his boot that it was

heading in my direction. And I knew that this would be my first big moment in an Ireland jersey.

The ball seemed to take forever to come down. It was probably only a few seconds, but it seemed like minutes. I could feel every set of eyes in the stadium staring at me as I looked up into the sky and waited . . .

'Okay,' I told myself, 'this is it! Concentrate, Gordon! And don't mess this up!'

I remembered what Jimmy O'Connor taught me to do when I played for Wexford Wanderers: 'Forget what's going on around you and just focus on the ball!'

I turned my body sideways, without ever taking my eyes off the ball. Then I put my hands in the air. The whole stadium seemed to go quiet as the ball fell . . .

Spinning . . .

Spinning . . .

Spinning . . .

And then . . .

BOOOMP!

I caught it! I caught it cleanly!

But I didn't have time to start congratulating myself. It was all very well catching the ball, but now there were four or five French players charging towards me and I knew I had to DO something with it.

I put my head down and I kicked it as hard as I could. It sailed over the heads of the French players and rolled out of play five metres from the French line. With my first kick of the game I had won a lineout, and for the first time I could actually hear the Irish fans in the stadium. They were singing:

'OLÉ, OLÉ, OLÉ, OLÉ! IRELAND! IRELAND!'

ROG slapped me on the back and said, 'Good catch, boy!'

BOD shouted, 'Well done, Darce!'

Paulie said, 'Good man – you're an Ireland player now!'

And something kind of amazing happened then. The nerves left me. It was like my body knew that I didn't have time to be worried – because there was a job to do.

The first half passed in a blur. There was so much happening. We had the ball and they chased us. Then they had the ball and we chased them. I ran around the place, putting out fires everywhere.

It was tackle . . .

. . . after tackle . . .

. . . after tackle . . .

. . . after tackle.

And then the referee blew his whistle and Brian said to me, 'That's it, Darce!'

'What?' I asked. 'Did I do something wrong?'

I thought I'd given away a penalty.

'No,' he said. 'It's half-time!'

Already? If only forty minutes passed that quickly at school, I thought.

The score was 12–12.

We walked back to the dressing room, where Warren was waiting to give us our instructions for the second half. He seemed pleased with how things were going, but at the same time he was cautious.

'Keep your concentration,' he said. 'Especially you, Darce. You need to watch out for Bastareaud. He's going to come on strong in the second half. And all he needs is one opportunity. So just make sure you don't give it to him. He has the measure of you now – we don't have the element of surprise anymore.'

I drank some water. I caught my breath. I compared war wounds with some of my teammates. I had a sore thigh. Paulie had a black eye. ROG had a dead leg. Strings had bruising to his ribs on both sides.

'Okay, forty minutes more!' Warren shouted. He clapped his two big hands together. 'I want you to spend the next thirty minutes concentrating on not losing the match, then the last ten on winning it!'

Then half-time was over and we walked back out onto the pitch to the same deafening noise as before.

The second half went by even quicker than the first. We did what Warren told us. We concentrated on not losing.

France scored two penalties . . . but ROG scored one.

And with fifteen minutes to go, we were just 18–15 behind.

Then BOD drew two players towards him and passed the ball to me. I had space in front of me and I decided to just run and see how far I could carry it. The answer was about twenty metres until . . .

BANG!

I ran into Bastareaud's forearm.

I was instantly dazed. I knew I was about to fall on my face. But that's when I discovered, to my great surprise, that I still had the ball in my hands.

As I hit the ground, I noticed our winger, Tyrone Howe, standing a few feet away from me. And he was in a lot of space. In one quick movement, I offloaded the ball to him. He caught it, then he set off down the field at a serious gallop.

I wondered if he had the legs to reach the line before the French players caught up with him. He kept pumping his legs and a few seconds later he crashed over the line.

And the Irish fans in the stadium went absolutely wild. The noise was almost deafening.

'YEEESSS!!!' I screamed. But I couldn't hear my own voice.

ROG added the conversion, and we were suddenly leading by 22–18 with twenty-five minutes of the second half gone.

We had fifteen minutes left to stop France from scoring a try. It was all hands on deck. The French were throwing the ball around, looking for openings in our defence. But we managed to keep them out.

Then, with just thirty seconds to go, Bastareaud got the ball in his hands. He put his head down and started moving towards the line like a runaway steamroller.

He was twenty yards from the line . . .

Then fifteen . . .

Then ten . . .

Then five . . .

I remembered what BOD had said to me before the match. And then he suddenly appeared out of nowhere and hit Bastareaud hard around the midriff. Bastareaud wobbled like a giant stack of Jenga pieces. I launched myself at him and applied the finish . . .

Down he went, knocking the ball forward. We had managed to keep France out. Seconds later, the game was over.

We celebrated with what little energy we had left in us.

ROG looked at my nose and he laughed.

'The good news is that your picture is going to be in all the papers tomorrow,' he said. 'The bad news is that your face is a mess!'

I had never felt so tired in my life. I could just about find the strength to raise my hands above my head and applaud the Irish supporters who had travelled to Paris to watch the match.

I felt a pat on the back. When I turned around, it was Bastareaud. He shook my hand and he said:

*'Vous avez le cœur d'un lion!'*[4]

Obviously, I had no idea what he was talking about. But I got the impression that it might have been a compliment.

---

[4] 'You have the heart of a lion!'

# 20 *Man of the Match*

Ryle Nugent was grinning from ear to ear.

'Gordon D'Arcy!' he said. 'That was one of the most impressive debuts ever seen from someone in an Ireland jersey! Sum up your thoughts for the nation, please!'

Sum up my thoughts for the nation? How could I? It had all happened so quickly. And now I was so tired that my head was empty.

Ryle pushed the microphone towards me. I sort of shuffled uneasily from foot to foot.

'I don't know *what* I feel,' I said. 'Relief, I suppose, that I didn't let anyone down.'

'Far from it!' said Ryle. 'You looked totally assured out there from the first minute, when you caught that ball and set up an attacking lineout.'

'Well, I just tried to remember one of the first

lessons I learned from Jimmy O'Connor when I started playing the game at Wexford Wanderers – forget what's going on around you and focus on the ball!'

I wish I could have forgotten what was going on around me at that moment. *And* who was looking at me! I was terrified talking in front of the camera, knowing that so many people back home in Ireland were likely to be watching.

'You took one hell of a bang to the face in the second half,' Ryle said, 'but you still managed to set up Tyrone Howe's match-winning try! And you stopped Mathieu Bastareaud from scoring right at the death! Do you think that makes you an automatic pick for the next match against Scotland in a fortnight's time?'

I hadn't even thought about it. As a matter of fact, I was so focused on not messing up against France that I'd somehow convinced myself it was a one-off, that I'd go back to Clongowes tomorrow night and my life would return to normal.

'Right now,' I told him, 'the only thing I'm thinking about is school on Monday morning and the two essays I'm supposed to have written about the Life Cycle of an Earthworm and the Causes of the First World War.'

Ryle laughed.

'Well,' he said, 'I don't know how you're going to come down from this high to go back to boring old schoolwork! But in today's test, I'm happy to tell you, you got an A-Plus! Gordon D'Arcy, you are the RTÉ Television Six Nations Man of the Match!'

Did he just say what I thought he said? Man of the Match? Seriously? Me?

He handed me a crystal vase. I was so shocked that I very nearly dropped it. Can you imagine how embarrassing that would have been? To have caught a high ball in the first minute, then let the Man of the Match award slip through my fingers.

I mumbled some thanks. Then I said, 'Can I just say hello to my mum and dad? And my brother Ian and my sisters, Shona and Megan? They're watching at home in Wexford.'

'No, we're not,' a voice behind me said.

'No!' I thought. 'No WAY!'

But there was no mistaking that voice . . .

It was Dad!

I turned around and he was standing there. And beside him was Mum. And Ian. And Shona and Megan.

Mum and Dad threw their arms around me and hugged me tightly.

'We're so proud of you!' Dad said.

'Our little Gordon!' Mum added.

I was in tears.

'You didn't tell me you were coming!' I said. 'You should have told me you were coming!'

'We didn't want to put more pressure on you,' Dad said. 'And we wanted it to be a surprise.'

It was certainly that.

'Well done,' Ian said. 'When I saw you hit Bastareaud, I said to Shona, "All those times he let me use him as a tackle bag – they really paid off in the end!"'

I laughed. I was so happy that they were there to see me play for Ireland. It made it the perfect day. In that moment, I said to myself that if I never played another rugby match, it wouldn't bother me at all. I'd be happy with this.

I told my mum that I wanted her to have my Man of the Match award. She said it would go lovely on the mantelpiece. She might even put daffodils in it.

'Oh, Gordon,' she said, 'you've made us the proudest parents in the world!'

'But the biggest challenge is yet to come,' Dad added.

'Do you mean Scotland in a two weeks' time?' I wondered. 'Because I'm not even thinking that far into the future.'

'Your dad is talking about you keeping your head,' Mum said. 'After what's happened over the past week, it would be very easy for you to get carried away with it all. We know what you're like, Gordon.'

'That's right,' Dad added. 'Just remember, don't go losing the run of yourself!'

Mums and dads are some of the cleverest people in the world. It's a wonder that we don't listen to them more often.

# 21 *Those Slippery Snails*

There was a banquet that night for the Irish and French players in a restaurant on the most famous street in Paris – the Champs-Élysées.

The match was over, which meant we could finally relax and enjoy ourselves. I chatted with some of the French players. And while I struggled to understand what they were saying, ROG very helpfully translated it for me.

'*Vous êtes un très bon joueur,*'[1] said Imanol Harinordoquy.

'He's asking if you're still in school,' ROG said.

'Yes,' I answered, nodding my head eagerly. 'I am. Yes, you're absolutely right.'

---

[1] 'You are a very good player!'

Everyone seemed to find this funny. I didn't know why.

There were no menus. We were all expected to eat exactly the same thing. But when the first course arrived, I couldn't BELIEVE what I was seeing. When the plate was put in front of me, I turned to BOD and said, 'Er, I think there's been some kind of mistake. I seem to have been given a plateful of snails.'

BOD laughed. 'Yeah, that's what they eat over here,' he told me.

'Snails?' I asked.

'They're considered a delicacy.'

'By humans?'

'Yes, by humans!'

'Not birds?'

'No, not birds! They're called *escargots*. Try them. They're nice.'

'Not a chance!'

The manager of the restaurant appeared at the table.

'*Tout va bien?*'[2] he asked, staring at me.

'He wants to know if you've a problem with the food?' ROG said.

[2] 'Are you okay?'

'Oh,' I replied. 'It's just that I've never eaten snails and I'm not sure that I want to start now.'

The manager nodded his head and said, *'Attendez! Je vais vous donner des pépites de poulet!'*[3] Then he strode off in the direction of the kitchen.

'What did he say?' I asked.

'He's not happy,' ROG said. 'I think you've insulted him. He said the French have been eating snails for centuries and who do you think you are coming in here and insulting his food like that? He said his restaurant has won all sorts of awards and has two Michelin stars. And that George Clooney

---

[3] 'Wait! I will get you some chicken nuggets!'

has his dinner here every time he's in Paris – and he always has the snails.'

'He said all of that? He didn't seem to be talking for that long.'

'Maybe you should just eat one,' Brian suggested. 'You might like them.'

I didn't want to offend the manager, so I decided to give it a go. Next to my plate, there was a strange device that looked like the forceps that Uncle Tim sometimes used to deliver the lambs. I looked at Paulie, who was making rapid progress through his plateful, so I copied him.

My stomach turned at the thought of eating a snail. Still, I picked up the shell using the forceps, then I tried to prise the thing out using the narrow fork I'd been given. But I must have squeezed too hard on the shell, because suddenly, without warning, it shot out of the forceps and bounced across the table, and landed in Mathieu Bastareaud's lap.

'*Zut alors!*'[4] he exclaimed.

'Knock on,' Strings said. 'Scrum, blue team.'

The French players all laughed. Strings was very funny.

Just as I was about to apologize to Bastareaud, the

---

[4] 'Oh, heck!'

manager returned with a plate of chicken nuggets and chips and placed them in front of me.

'*Bon appétit!*' he said – and that I definitely *did* understand.

Everyone laughed. And I had to laugh, too. My teammates had well and truly suckered me!

After dinner, we all went to visit the Eiffel Tower. It was the most spectacular sight I had ever seen. It was made up of thousands of lengths of irons all bolted together. And it was three hundred and twenty-four metres high, which made it roughly the size of three rugby pitches laid end to end.

'Let's go up in it,' Paulie said. 'We'll be able to see the whole city at night.'

Everyone agreed and started walking towards it, even though I had a secret that I decided to keep to myself for now. I was TERRIFIED of heights!

But, not for the first time recently, I decided to just face my fear.

We queued for the lifts. Each lift was supposed to be capable of carrying twenty people. But as soon as eight members of the Ireland pack got in, the lift operator announced that we had reached the maximum weight capacity and the rest of us would have to wait for the next lift.

Eventually, we climbed into the next lift and it

shuddered its way slowly to the top of the tower. I stood with my back to the glass, staring up, so that I wouldn't have to watch the ground disappear below our feet.

At the top, we got out of the lift and, when I saw how high up we were, my legs felt weak. But I plucked up the courage to look, and the view was spectacular. It was nearly midnight and the lights of Paris sparkled below us and stretched out as far as the eye could see.

ROG patted me on the back and said, 'You did great today, boy.'

I peered over the edge and I said, 'It's a long way down, isn't it?'

I didn't realize how true those words would prove to be.

# 22 'LE-GEND!'

We arrived back in Dublin the following afternoon. There was a bus waiting at the airport to bring us to the Shelbourne Hotel in Dublin City Centre, where most of the players had their cars parked. Warren asked the driver to take a long detour through Kildare to make sure I was dropped off at the gates of the school.

I said goodbye to my new teammates, not knowing whether I'd be seeing them again. Although I'd won the Man of the Match award, I didn't dare presume that I'd be in the squad for the next match.

The bus pulled up on the road outside the school. As I walked past his seat, Warren called me back.

'Gordon,' he said, 'what are you doing next weekend?'

'Er, same as usual,' I said. 'I'll be here in the school.'

'Will you come and train with us again next Saturday?'

'I'd love to!'

'You did a good job,' he said. 'And I want you in the squad for the Scotland match.'

With my bag slung over my shoulder, I walked up the long driveway to the school feeling ten feet tall. What happened in Paris suddenly felt like the beginning of something rather than just one day when I got lucky.

The sun was shining, the birds were singing and all was good with the world.

In the distance, I noticed that the St Bridget's girls were using our pitch again. They were playing a match among themselves – fifteen against fifteen. I spotted Aoife. She was hard to miss. She had the ball in her hands. She kicked for touch, then she started shouting instructions at the girls in the lineout.

I made my way over to the pitch and watched them for a little while. They were very good. I thought to myself that our school team could learn a few things from the quick way they moved the ball around.

Soon, the whistle blew and their training match was over. I watched them shake hands with each other. Then Aoife spotted me standing on the sideline.

'Hi, Gordon!' she said. 'I saw the match on TV. You were amazing.'

I remembered what Dad had said about keeping my head and not losing the run of myself.

'Thanks,' I said. 'The most important thing is that the team won.'

She was spinning a rugby ball around in her hands.

'So come on,' she said, 'let me see it!'

'See what?' I asked.

'Your Ireland jersey, of course!'

I reached into my bag and pulled it out. It was screwed up in a ball. I handed it to Aoife and she opened it out to get a proper look at it. She stared at the crest.

'Oh my God!' she said. 'That is *so* cool!'

'You can have it,' I said. 'That's if you want it.'

'I'm not taking your Ireland jersey! It's yours!'

She turned it over and saw the word 'D'Arcy' on the back.

'Wow!' she exclaimed. 'That! Is! Amazing!'

'Hey, I was watching you play,' I said. 'You're a really good team.'

'Thank you,' Aoife replied. 'We're getting there. We're playing our first match in a few weeks' time. Against St Theresa's.'

'That's exciting.'

'Some of the girls could do with some individual
skills coaching – just to cut down on the handling
errors.'

'Maybe I could help them with that.'

'What? Really?'

'Yeah. As a matter of fact, I could do a training
session with you,' I said.

'Well, it'd be great for them to work with an *actual*
Ireland international! Thanks so much!'

'It'd be a pleasure.'

'What about Friday after school?'

'Friday after school works for me.'

She was still holding my Ireland jersey. 'Maybe I could borrow this?' she said. 'I just want to show it to my mum and dad. Just to prove that I *do* actually know you.'

'To *prove* it?' I asked.

'We were watching the match on Saturday and I told them that I'd tackled you a few weeks ago and knocked you flat on your face.'

'You're still kind of proud of that, aren't you?'

'It's my claim to fame now! Except they think I'm making it up.'

'Okay,' I said, 'you take the jersey and we'll call it a loan.'

She folded it up delicately, like it was something very, very precious.

'I'll see you next Friday,' I told her.

Then we said goodbye and I headed for the school building. I thought I'd go to the dorm to catch an hour or two of sleep. Then I'd go to the library for a few hours to work. Those two essays weren't going to write themselves. That was the plan anyway. But when I walked into the school, I couldn't believe the scene that awaited me in the lobby.

185

There were five hundred students waiting to greet me. And when I walked in, they burst into a loud cheer.

I picked out the faces of Conor and Peter in the crowd. They were clapping me, along with everyone else.

There was a huge banner hanging from one side of the lobby to the other. It said: 'Congratulations, Gordon D'Arcy! Clongowes is Proud of You!'

Then they started singing. They started singing *that* song:

> *Mill 'em, Darce!*
> *Na na na!*
> *Mill 'em, Darce!*
> *Na na na!*
> *You better hope and pray*
> *You don't get in his way,*
> *Mill 'em, Darce!*
> *Na na na!*

It was immediately clear that this was one hundred times bigger than scoring the try that beat the Blackrock Dream Team!

Mr Murray stepped forward.

'Well done, Gordon,' he said. 'I knew from the

first time I saw you play that there was something special about you. We're all very, very proud of you at this school.'

'Thanks, Mr Murray,' I said. 'It never would have happened if you hadn't taken a chance on me against Blackrock.'

'You're a great rugby player, Gordon. And, difficult as it is, you're going to have to keep this wonderful thing that's happened to you in perspective. By all means enjoy it. But don't let it go to your head, okay?'

I felt myself being lifted off my feet, then hoisted onto the shoulders of two other boys. And then I was being carried around the corridors of the school by a crowd of students, who were chanting:

'LE-GEND! LE-GEND! LE-GEND! LE-GEND!'

And looking back, if I was to pinpoint the exact moment when I started to lose the run of myself, then that was probably it.

## 23 *Star Power*

It was the following morning. I didn't know what time it was, but I awoke with a sudden start. I sat bolt upright in my bed with that terrible feeling you get when you're sure there was something you were meant to do, but you can't remember what that something was.

And then it hit me . . .

'MY ESSAYS!' I screamed.

Conor and Peter were already up and dressed.

'You didn't *do* them?' Peter asked. 'But they were assigned nearly two weeks ago!'

'I was *going* to do them yesterday,' I said. 'But then there was the big Welcome Home party. It must have just slipped my mind.'

'What slipped your mind?' Flash Barry said, returning from the bathroom at that exact moment.

'My essays,' I said. 'I had two of them to write. One about the Life Cycle of an Earthworm and the other about the Causes of the First World War.'

'I wouldn't worry about it,' he said.

'What do you mean, I wouldn't worry about it? We've got History this morning! Mr Boyce will go BANANAS when I tell him that I don't have anything for him!'

'You *do* have something for him.'

He picked up my History copybook from my study table and handed it to me.

'There you go,' he said.

I flicked through the pages. And there it was – an essay on the Causes of the First World War, complete with bulletpoints.

Teachers LOVE bulletpoints.

'Eight hundred words exactly,' Barry said.

The strangest thing of all was that it seemed to be written in my handwriting.

'But I didn't do this,' I said. 'Unless I was sleep-writing? Is sleep-writing an actual thing?'

'I did it,' Barry said. 'I'm quite good at forging other people's handwriting.'

'Wow,' I said, very impressed. 'Did you write the essay as well?'

'No,' he said. 'I copied Peter's.'

'*What?*' Peter said. He wasn't happy. 'You shouldn't have done that. It's cheating.'

'Cheating?' Barry said. 'I thought Darce here was supposed to be your friend?'

'He *is* my friend,' said Peter. 'We've known each other since we were five years old.'

'Then you shouldn't mind helping him out. Unless you're not happy for him – for all the success that's suddenly come his way?'

'Of course I'm happy for him,' Peter said. 'I'm just worried that Mr Boyce will notice the similarities between our essays.'

'That's why I changed a word here and there,' Barry explained. 'Look, Darce is an international rugby player now. He shouldn't have to worry about things like homework.'

I thought about what he was saying for a moment. He sort of had a point.

'Yeah,' I said, 'there's also the other essay I mentioned. The one on the Life Cycle of an Earthworm.'

'And *that's* done, too,' he said, picking up my Science copybook from the study table and putting it into my hands. 'Check it out – there's diagrams and everything with it.'

I flicked through it. He was right. I'd get an A for this. No doubt about it.

Peter frowned. 'You didn't copy my earthworm essay as well, did you?'

'Of course I didn't,' Barry said. 'I'm not stupid. I copied Conor's.'

'*What?*' Conor said. He wasn't happy either.

Barry pointed at me. 'This is Gordon D'Arcy!' he said. 'He's got a Six Nations Championship to think about! He shouldn't have to concern himself with schoolwork!'

'Yeah,' Conor said, 'but what if Mr Dockrell notices that his essay is the same as mine?'

'Again,' Barry said, 'I changed bits of it here and there. You're definitely Darce's friend, are you?'

'Of course I'm his friend!'

'It's just, you don't seem to be acting like a friend. It's like you're not pleased for him or something. Anyone would think you were jealous of him!'

'I'm not jealous of him. I'm thrilled for him.'

'Darce,' Barry said, 'you just stay focused on the Scotland match and leave the homework for someone else to do.'

I threw back my duvet. 'I suppose I'd better get up,' I said.

It was time for breakfast.

I found my shirt, trousers and jumper and I put them on. Then I went looking for my blazer, but I couldn't find it anywhere. I noticed that Barry was holding it up for me to put my arms into it – kind of like a butler would.

'Thank you,' I said as I slipped my arms inside the sleeves.

'You're welcome,' he said, picking specks of fluff from my shoulders.

We headed for the cafeteria. I walked with Barry while Conor and Peter followed a few steps behind us.

The corridors were crowded with boys. But this morning I didn't need to zigzag my way through them like I usually did. The crowds parted as if I was driving a bus through them. And everyone stared at me with their mouths open.

'Seriously,' I said, 'why are they all looking at me like that?'

'Because,' Barry replied, 'you're famous now. This is called star power.'

'It feels kind of weird,' I said.

'Well, you'd better get used to it. Because this is your life now.'

We reached the cafeteria. We were late. And the queue was SERIOUSLY long. It would take us twenty minutes to get our breakfast at this rate.

'Look at the queue,' I said. 'There won't be time for us to eat a thing before the bell goes.'

'*You* don't have to queue,' Barry said, then he put his hand on my back and steered me to the top of the line. No one objected to us skipping them.

I looked over my shoulder. Conor and Peter had taken their place at the back of the queue.

Janice, the chief dinner lady, was standing there in her chef's outfit. She didn't look up.

'What do you want?' she said.

'Can I have two sausages —' I started to ask, but she cut me off.

'We're running low on sausages,' she said. 'The most anyone is allowed today is —'

But then she looked up and forgot what she'd been saying. She stared at me like she was seeing a ghost.

'Oh, it's you!' she said. Her face reddened. 'I saw you on the television!'

'It's, er, Gordon,' I told her.

'My husband said, "You watch this kid! He's going to be one of the greatest players ever to play for Ireland!" What'll it be, love?'

'Er, can I have one sausage —'

'*One* sausage?' she said, like I was being ridiculous. 'You'll have more than one sausage!'

'I thought you said the most anyone was allowed this morning was —'

'For that lot, yes. Not for you. You need your strength. You can't play rugby for Ireland eating one sausage a day. What do you think my husband would say if he was watching the television and you suddenly fell down weak with the hunger? He'd say, "What have you been feeding him in that school, Janice?" I can't turn around and tell him, "Oh, I think that's my fault – I only gave him one sausage."'

'Well,' I said guiltily, 'could I have *two* sausages, then?'

I absolutely LOVED sausages.

'You can have ten if you want! Or twenty!'

'Have twenty,' Barry suggested.

'Em, twenty does sound kind of good,' I agreed. I was really hungry. 'And some beans – if there's any room left.'

She filled my plate, then I found a table and sat down. Barry sat down opposite me. As I tucked into my sausages and a mountain of beans, he reached into his inside pocket and pulled out a small piece of card.

'I took the liberty of running off a few hundred of these on the school photocopier,' he said. 'I hope you don't mind.'

'What is it?' I asked.

He put it on the table in front of me. It was a business card. On it, in gold writing, it said:

**FLASH BARRY SPORTS MANAGEMENT**

And then, underneath, in black:

**Barry Considine**
**Agent To The Stars**

'I'm offering you my services,' he said. 'I'm giving you the chance to become my very first client.'

'Barry,' I said, 'I already told you, I don't *need* an agent.'

'I think things have moved on quite a bit since we had that conversation, don't you?'

'What do you mean?'

'Darce, look at the way people are staring at you! You're in the Big League now! You need someone to look after you – the way I looked after you this morning! Doing your homework for you! Bringing you to the top of the queue! Getting you all those sausages!'

'I don't know, Barry.'

'How would you like to go to the premiere of the new James Bond movie?'

'What? Seriously?'

'It's on in the Savoy. My dad can get us tickets. He's an agent, too. He represents a lot of actors.'

'Oh my God, I've never been to a movie premiere before.'

'Hey, they're great fun. You'll be rubbing shoulders with some major stars.'

'When did you say it was on?'

'Friday night. I was thinking we could get the bus to Dublin as soon as the last class of the day is over.'

I suddenly remembered something.

'Oh, I've got this other *thing* on,' I said.

'What thing?' he asked.

'I promised this friend of mine – her name's Aoife – that I'd help her with something.'

'You're going to turn down an invitation to a movie premiere to hang out with a *girl*?'

'It's not so much to hang out with her,' I told him. 'I told her I'd give her team some coaching tips.'

'Coaching tips?' he said, looking at me like I was mad. 'Are you kidding me?'

'Well, no,' I said. 'They're playing their first match soon, against St Theresa's. I told Aoife I'd show them how to cut down on their handling errors.'

'What am I going to do with you? For God's sake – YOU'RE GORDON D'ARCY! And you're giving away coaching tips FOR FREE? You've got to think bigger, Darce! You know what I'd love to see you doing for the Easter holidays? How does this sound: Gordon D'Arcy's Rugby School of Excellence!'

'It sounds, I don't know, good, I suppose.'

'This is why you need me in your corner, Darce!'

'Maybe you're right.'

'So what do you say? Are you going to let me be your agent?'

I looked up and I noticed Conor and Peter still in the breakfast queue, staring at me disapprovingly.

'Okay,' I said. 'Why not?'

'You're not going to regret this,' said Barry. 'I can promise you that.'

## 24  *Crowd Pleaser*

I'm going to be honest here – after my heroics for Ireland against France, playing rugby with boys my own age suddenly felt like it was beneath me. I had experienced rugby at the very highest level and playing with my fellow First Years at Free Time that Monday was a serious comedown for me.

But, as I explained to Conor and Peter as we got changed into our rugby gear, I had been lucky enough to get the call-up for Ireland and I didn't mind giving something back, even if that meant sharing a pitch with players who clearly weren't in my class.

'That's, em, not a very nice thing to say,' Peter said.

It was still true, though.

The other reason it was important for me to play

was that a lot of boys had turned up to watch me – a couple of hundred of them, as a matter of fact. Many of them had probably never seen an Ireland rugby international up close before, so this was a major deal for them.

Plus, as Barry said, 'It'll be good for your image to be seen as the kind of player who occasionally lowers himself to play with mere mortals.'

Mr Murray emptied the high-viz jackets out onto the ground. Everyone waited to see what colour I chose because they all wanted to be on the same side. I chose yellow. Then the rest of them dived on top of the pile to try to get their hands on a yellow one.

I was glad to see that Peter and Conor would both be on my team, although they would be expected to work hard. As good as I was, I couldn't afford to carry any passengers.

Mr Murray suggested that we warm up with some light jogging, back-pedalling and shuffling from side to side.

'Are we going to be doing any running and passing drills?' I asked as I jogged beside him.

'Any what?' he said.

'Running and passing drills,' I repeated. 'We did them when I trained with the Ireland team.'

'Well, you're not training with the Ireland team now,' he reminded me.

'I get you,' I said. Obviously he meant that the other boys wouldn't be able for the intensity.

'When you're training for Warren, you do what Warren tells you,' he said. 'When you're training for me, you do what I tell you. Do you understand?'

'I do, Mr Murray. The fitness at international level is so much higher.'

We warmed up. Then the match began. The yellows against the oranges. I wanted to play well because I could feel every set of eyes around the pitch focused on me.

I gave the crowd what they wanted. Exhibition stuff mostly. No-look passes. Back-handed passes. Over-my-shoulder passes. Through-my-legs passes. The crowd cheered my every touch.

Unfortunately, not everyone was having the kind of game that I was enjoying. Peter was having a nightmare. Every time he got the ball in his hands, he passed it to one of the opposition players, until I eventually had to shout at him:

'For God's sake, Peter, what is wrong with you today?'

'I'm sorry,' he said. 'I'm just a bit nervous with all these people watching.'

'It's a couple of hundred people,' I said. 'Try playing at the Stade de France in Paris in front of a hundred thousand. *That's* pressure.'

'My passing is a bit off today, that's all.'

'Maybe you should start wearing contact lenses when you're playing. You're dragging us down here, Peter.'

Conor tried to reason with me. 'Calm down, Gordon,' he said. 'It's just a friendly match.'

'There's no such thing as a friendly match in rugby,' I told him. 'That's why all matches are called Tests. I think Peter is focused on the other kind of tests – his summer exams. He needs to get his head in the game.'

'Gordon, I think you're being a bit hard on him.'

'If he played like that for Ireland, Conor, he'd be taken off. No arguments. And you would as well, by the way. You're having an absolute shocker today.'

'I'm enjoying myself,' he said. 'That's the reason I play rugby.'

It wasn't the attitude of a winner. All I could do was just shake my head.

We played on. We scored four unanswered tries against the orange team. I scored two of them and made the decisive pass for the other two. Meanwhile, the crowd continued to applaud every time I performed one of my little tricks.

I was box office. There was no question about that. But at half-time, Mr Murray asked me if he could have a word with me.

'Yeah, sure,' I said. 'What's up?'

'Look, take this as constructive criticism,' he said, 'but you're being a bit of a show-off out there.'

'Hey,' I said, 'the people came here today to be entertained, and I'm only too happy to oblige.'

'But rugby is a gentleman's game, Gordon. It's not enough to be the best. You have to play the game in the right spirit. Which means, even if you're great, you don't rub the opposition's nose in it like you have been doing today. And you don't humiliate a teammate just because he's having a bad day.'

'I'll take that on board.'

'You should definitely do that.'

'I said I would.'

But in the second half, I continued with the same antics. I made fools of the orange players. I intercepted a bad pass and I ran on to score a try, crossing the line running backwards and sticking my tongue out at the player who was chasing back after me.

The crowd loved every minute of it.

But then, with a few minutes to go, Conor did something unforgivable – and he did it to try to make me look bad in front of everyone. There was a break in play while one of our players limped off after twisting his ankle.

'Come on, yellow team,' I shouted, 'let's not ease off, even though we're seventy points ahead!'

And that's when Conor did it. He crept up behind me – and he pulled down my shorts.

Everyone on the sideline laughed. So did the opposition players. And my own teammates.

I quickly pulled them up again, then I gave Conor a shove in the chest.

'What do you think you're doing?' I asked.

'It was just a joke,' he said. 'Lighten up, Gordon.'

'No, I won't lighten up.'

'I'm just having a laugh. You know me.'

'Yeah, I do know you. And maybe that's why I got to play for Ireland and you never will.'

I knew in that moment that I'd hurt his feelings. But honestly, I didn't care.

Mr Murray blew his whistle. 'I think we'll leave it there,' he said.

'What are you talking about?' I asked him. 'There's at least ten minutes left.'

'You're seventy points ahead, Gordon.'

'But we could score more. The crowd are loving it.'

'No.' Mr Murray said. 'It's over.'

I looked at Conor and Peter. They were looking at me and shaking their heads.

'You've changed,' Peter said.

I shrugged. 'For the better – I hope.'

## 25  *Man of the Moment*

The path in front of the Savoy was packed with people. They were all straining to get a look at the celebrities who'd turned up to see the premiere of the new James Bond movie.

I heard someone say they saw Bono go in. And Michael Flatley from *Riverdance*.

Barry patted the pocket of his blazer.

'I've got the tickets,' he said, as we squeezed through the crowds.

There were two entrances to the Savoy. One was for was celebrities, the other for non-celebrities. I went to take the second entrance, but Barry called me back.

'Where are you going?' he asked.

'Er, into the cinema,' I said.

'That entrance is for ordinary people.'

'I know.'

He laughed. 'You still don't get it,' he said. 'You're not an ordinary person anymore! You don't want to sneak into a celebrity premiere unseen. You want people to KNOW you're here. Come with me.'

I followed him to the celebrity entrance. There was a big, burly bouncer in a tuxedo standing in front of the door, barring our way.

'I've got Gordon D'Arcy here!' Barry told him.

It was as if he'd said some magic password because the bouncer immediately stepped aside and said, 'Enjoy your evening, Mr D'Arcy.'

Inside, there was a long, red carpet stretching out in front of me. And to the right of it was a wall of faces — dozens and dozens of journalists, photographers and TV crews, who were barking out questions at people walking along the carpet.

Questions like:

'What are you wearing?'

And:

'Are you looking forward to the movie?'

I looked at Barry.

'Off you go,' he said.

I took a step backwards.

'No way!' I said.

'Darce,' he said, 'trust me, okay? You have to accept

the fact that you're a very big deal now. You're more famous than most of the people who've walked that carpet tonight – with the exception of Bono, and possibly Michael Flatley from *Riverdance*.'

'I don't know, Barry.'

'Darce, you deserve this. You've earned it.'

He put his hand on my back and gave me a shove of encouragement. I stepped onto the carpet.

I heard someone shout, 'There's Gordon D'Arcy – the rugby player!' and suddenly I was blinded by camera flashes. Twenty or thirty microphones were thrust in my face. Then the questions started:

'What are you wearing?'

'It's, er, just my school uniform,' I said. 'Clongowes Wood College.'

'Who's it by?'

'Er, I don't know. I think my mum bought it in Arnotts.'

'So that look *is* available on the High Street?'

'Er, I suppose so, yeah.'

'Tell us, how does it feel to be Irish rugby's Man of the Moment?'

'Good, I suppose.'

'Tell us about the pass you made for the winning try against France.'

'Well,' I said, 'it was nothing really –'

Then I heard Barry's voice coming from behind the wall of reporters and photographers.

'It was far from nothing,' he said loudly. 'My client is being modest. It's something I'm trying to coach out of him.'

Everyone laughed.

'There were ten minutes of the match left,' Barry said, 'and Ireland were behind. Most of the Irish players had given up – but this man hadn't. I mean, that's not the Gordon D'Arcy way. And, yes, he had to grab one or two of his teammates by the scruff of the neck and say, "GUYS, WE'RE NOT BEATEN YET! WE CAN STILL WIN THIS THING!"'

I watched all of their faces warm to the story. There was no doubt that Barry told it better than me – even if all of the details were completely untrue.

'What happened then?' a reporter asked.

'Gordon knew that if something was going to happen, he was going to have to make it happen himself. He carried the ball a good thirty, forty metres. Then he saw Mathieu Bastareaud CHARGING towards him with a face full of FURY. He saw his elbow heading straight for his nose. But he thought to himself, "Just take the hit, Darce! Take it for the team!" And that's when he felt it. BANG! It was like he'd been hit by a train!'

'Can we quote you on that?' a reporter said to me.

I shrugged. 'I suppose so,' I said.

'He felt his entire nose move,' Barry continued. 'He could feel the bone CRUNCH. And yet even then his first thought was, "Hey, forget your looks, Darce! You can always have plastic surgery later on! The important thing is that you keep the ball alive!" As he hit the deck, he noticed that Tyrone Howe was standing in the far-off distance. But he knew that if he was going to get the ball to him . . . it was going to take one HELL of a pass. Gordon, do you want to take over the story from here? Tell them what happened next.'

'I threw the ball to Tyrone Howe,' I said, 'and he scored a try.'

'Brilliant story!' a TV reporter said to me. 'Enjoy the movie, Gordon!'

I walked the rest of the red carpet, posing for a few photographs along the way. Barry met me at the other end. He handed me a giant bucket of nachos, which were smothered in cheese sauce.

'Here you go,' he said.

'I wonder should I be eating things like this?' I said.

'You'll be fine,' Barry assured me. 'You can run it off at training this weekend. And, by the way, we definitely need to work on your skills as storyteller!'

When the movie was over, we took a taxi back to Clongowes. I don't know how much it cost, but Barry said he'd look after it and I could pay him back once the money started rolling in. I wasn't quite sure *how* money was going to roll in, but I was too tired to ask.

When we got back to the dorm, the room was in darkness. Peter was fast asleep and snoring as usual:

HOOOCCCKKK . . . ZZZUUUUUU!!!!!!

HOOOCCCKKK . . . ZZZUUUUUU!!!!!!

HOOOCCCKKK . . . ZZZUUUUUU!!!!!!

'We've got to do something about that,' Barry said.

I changed into my pyjamas. And then, as I climbed the ladder and got into my coffin, I heard a voice below me say:

'So, how was the movie?'

It was Conor — and he sounded kind of sad.

'It was great,' I said. 'I walked the red carpet. You should have seen all the cameras and reporters there.'

He was silent for a little while, then he said, 'I was talking to my cousin, Aoife. She said you promised to do some coaching with her team tonight, but you never showed up. She was really upset, Darce.'

Out of the darkness came Barry's voice. 'If your cousin and her friends want to receive coaching tips from my client, they can sign up for Gordon D'Arcy's Rugby School of Excellence this Easter. Now, can you please let my client go to sleep? He's training with the Ireland rugby squad tomorrow.'

# 26  *Travelling in Style*

It was the following morning. I was standing with Barry outside the school, wondering how we were going to get to Greystones for training.

'It's all in hand,' he told me. 'These are the things you don't need to worry about when you have the best agent in the business!'

A moment later, our transport arrived. I couldn't believe what I was seeing.

Barry had ordered a stretch limo.

And it was HUGE!

'Have you ever been in one of these things before?' he asked.

'Er, no,' I said. The only time I'd ever seen one was on TV.

It was black. And it was polished to such a fine sheen that you could see your face reflected in the bonnet. The driver got out. He was wearing a chauffeur's uniform, complete with hat.

'Good morning, Mr D'Arcy,' he said as he opened the door for us.

'Go on, get in,' Barry said, grinning. 'You're going to love it.'

Weirdly, it seemed even bigger on the inside than it did on the outside. It was half the size of a rugby pitch — or so it seemed. The seats were made of cream-coloured leather. There was a mini fridge that was filled with every type of fizzy drink you could name. Plus, there was a cocktail shaker, so you could mix whatever you wanted:

'What'll it be?' Barry asked. 'Coke and Fanta? Fanta and 7-Up? 7-Up and Coke? Or why not all three?'

'No,' I said, remembering my conversation with BOD on the flight to Paris. 'I probably should stay hydrated. Are there any energy drinks in there?'

'Energy drinks? That's hilarious! I think if you proved anything in Paris, it's that you don't need energy drinks. You can drink whatever you want.'

'I suppose,' I said. 'Okay, I'll have all three, then!'

'Greystones,' Barry told the driver.

Actually, it was more like 'GREEEYYY-STOOONNNEEESSS!!!' because the driver was sitting a long way away.

'So what do you think?' Barry asked.

'It's the most incredible car I've ever seen,' I told him truthfully.

'Hey, get used to it!' he said. 'Because this is how superstars travel!'

I sat back and sipped my cocktail – I'd decided to name it a Cokanta-Up.

'There's something I need to talk to you about,' Barry said. 'It's a bit, em, delicate.'

'What is it?' I asked.

'I'm just going to come right out and say it. It's Conor.'

'Conor? As in, my friend Conor?'

'Well, that's the point – *is* he your friend?'

'Of course he's my friend!'

'It's just, all that stuff he was saying last night about his cousin being upset. You were in great form after the movie premiere. It was like he was trying to drag you down.'

'Do you think so?'

'That's what it sounded like to me. Look, there's going to be a lot of people who are very jealous of you, Darce. You need to cut those people out of your life.'

Outside the window, I saw a sign that read: 'Greystones – One Kilometre'.

I decided to change into my rugby gear in the back of the limo. I pulled on my jersey, shorts, socks and boots.

Then Barry handed me a small box.

'What's this?' I asked.

'A little gift,' he said.

I opened the box. It was a pair of sunglasses. I looked out the window. The sky was grey. Flecks of rain were starting to fall.

'I'm not sure if it's the right weather for these,' I said.

'You don't wear shades to keep the sun out of your eyes,' Barry said. 'You wear shades to let the world know that you're very, very important.'

'Right,' I said.

I put them on just as the limo pulled up in the car park. Barry got out and held open the door for me.

'Remember,' he said, 'you're more than just a rugby player, Darce – you're a superstar! Start acting like one, okay?'

I stepped out of the back of the car. All of my Ireland teammates were already on the field. Even through the dark glasses, I could see the looks on their faces. I thought they were impressed. I couldn't have been more wrong.

But I didn't find that out until much later.

217

## 27 *A Bit of a Belly*

'SCOTLAND ARE NOBODY'S MUGS! WE'RE GOING TO HAVE TO BE AT THE TOP OF OUR GAME IF WE'RE GOING TO BUILD ON WHAT WE ACHIEVED IN PARIS LAST WEEKEND!'

That wasn't Warren Gatland shouting, by the way. It wasn't ROG, or Paulie, or BOD.

It was me!

It was big, bold, overly confident, superstar-wannabe ME!

'I'VE BEEN THINKING ABOUT THIS QUITE A LOT,' I said. 'AND I'M CON-VINCED THAT THE KEY TO BEATING SCOTLAND ... IS GIVING ME PLENTY OF THE BALL!'

Warren Gatland just stared at me. 'Is that right?' he said.

'YOU BETTER BELIEVE IT!' I said. 'JUST GIVE THE BALL TO ME, LADS – AND LET ME WORK MY MAGIC!'

Everyone just stared at me.

'Darce,' the coach said, 'we have a rule here that says we take our sunglasses off when we're training.'

'Fair enough,' I said. I took them off and hung them on the front of my jersey.

I noticed then that a few of the players were staring at my midriff.

'What's wrong?' I asked.

It was Paulie who said what everyone else was thinking.

'Darce, you've a bit of a belly on you there. Have you been following the daily nutrition and training plan?'

I looked down and saw my stomach overhanging the waistband of my shorts.

All ROG could do was shake his head. 'What have you been eating?' he asked.

I didn't mention the sausages or the bucket of nachos with cheese sauce. Instead, I told them, 'I've been eating all the right foods – just in bigger

portions. The dinner lady at school insisted on giving me a little bit extra. She said I needed my strength.'

I looked at my teammates. They were all looking at me like they didn't believe a word I'd just said.

I grabbed the flabby folds of my belly in my two hands.

'The great thing about me,' I said, 'is that I can

run this off easily. Seriously, I'll train hard today, then I'll cut back on my portions next week.'

Warren clapped his hands together and said, 'Okay, guys, let's work!'

I trained well, performing all the drills, like:

Sprinting . . .

Passing and handling . . .

Hitting the tackle bag . . .

And I let my voice be heard as well. I wasn't shy when it came to shouting out instructions, like:

'ROG, YOU NEED TO GIVE ME QUICKER BALL THAN THAT!'

And:

'PAULIE, YOU NEED TO PUT YOUR WEIGHT IN AT RUCK TIME!'

And

'BRIAN, IF YOU DO THAT AGAINST SCOTLAND, THEY'RE GOING TO PUN-ISH US!'

I thought I was contributing in a positive way. A little bit of constructive criticism is good for us all, I figured.

Then we practised some set moves. Warren split the backs into groups of four to practise various attacking setpieces that we could perform off second phase ball. I was with BOD, ROG and Rob

Kearney. We practised the miss-pass, where four of you run in a diagonal line – but instead of passing to the player immediately next to you, you throw it long to the second player over. That can really confuse defences, especially if you can trick them into thinking you're going to throw a short pass.

We practised it about twenty times until I started to become a bit bored.

'Maybe we'll do something else now,' I suggested. 'I understand how this one works.'

ROG got annoyed with me. 'It's not about understanding it,' he said. 'It's about doing it over and over again until you can do it without even thinking about it. So that it's like a muscle memory.'

What was his problem? I wondered.

'Fine,' I said. 'Let's keep doing it.'

So we did it for another twenty minutes.

Then we practised the wrap switch, which is where the player who receives the pass suddenly changes the direction of his run, so that he runs into the space behind the player who passed to him. Again, this can really wrong-foot the opposition if they're expecting you to go one way and you go the other.

We practised this move over and over and over again. We must have done it a hundred times. Sometimes I was the player who changed the direction of the play, sometimes it was one of the others. We all took turns.

BOD was also a stickler for doing things right. He didn't want us to stop practising the move until we got it right ten times in a row. If we did it right six times in a row and then one of us dropped the ball, or knocked it on, or passed it forward, then the counter went back to zero again – and we had to get it right ten times again.

'The harder you work,' BOD said, 'the easier it gets.'

And they were both right. The more we practised the move, the more times it came off. The only problem was that I was starting to get tired. That's when I spotted Barry standing on the sideline. He was holding up a drink. He must have read my mind because I was thirsty. I jogged over to him.

'Made you another Cokanta-Up,' he said.

I took a sip.

'Hey,' he added, 'we might think of marketing that.'

'Marketing it?' I asked.

'Marketing it and selling it. Your own soft drink. Actually, while you've been out there training, I've been on the phone talking to various companies, trying to get you some endorsement deals.'

'What are endorsement deals?'

'Endorsement deals are money, Darce! For advertising things!'

'What kind of things would I be advertising?'

'Mobile phones. Watches. Sunglasses. Anything they're prepared to pay you to sell.'

'Seriously?'

'I told you, my dad does this for a living. And he always says that you only get a small window of opportunity in which to cash in. Fame doesn't last forever. You have to get out of it *what* you can, *while* you can.'

It was at that exact moment that Warren Gatland began shouting at me. He'd noticed that I'd separated myself from the other players and had stopped training.

'COME ON, DARCE!' he shouted. 'BACK TO WORK!'

'Tell him to get lost,' Barry said.

I couldn't believe what I was hearing.

'I can't do that!' I told him. 'He's the Ireland coach!'

'Trust me,' Barry said, 'he'll respect you more for it in the long run. Tell him you've worked hard enough for one day. You trained for nearly an hour.'

It was true. I *was* tired. Plus I was a bit burpy after

the two Cokanta-Ups I'd drunk. So I did what Barry suggested.

'I THINK I'VE DONE ENOUGH FOR TODAY!' I yelled at Warren.

'I'LL TELL YOU WHEN YOU'VE DONE ENOUGH!' Warren shouted back at me. 'GET BACK TO WORK!'

'Tell him you don't want to overtrain,' Barry said, 'and have nothing left in the tank for Scotland next weekend.'

'I DON'T WANT TO OVERTRAIN,' I told him, 'AND HAVE NOTHING LEFT IN THE TANK FOR SCOTLAND NEXT WEEK-END. PLUS I'M A BIT BURPY!'

Warren stared at me for a long moment.

'BURPY?' he asked.

'YES, BURPY!' I told him. 'I'VE HAD TWO COKANTA-UPS.'

'Say "Trademark Gordon D'Arcy Enterprises".'

'TRADEMARK GORDON D'ARCY EN-TERPRISES!'

'Tell him you're going back to school,' Barry said, 'to chill out.'

'I'M GOING BACK TO SCHOOL,' I said, 'TO CHILL OUT.'

I started walking with Barry towards the limo.

'COME BACK HERE NOW,' Warren ordered, 'AND TRAIN WITH THE REST OF YOUR TEAMMATES!'

'SORRY!' I told him. 'NO CAN DO!'

'GORDON, YOU'RE DISRESPECTING ME AND YOU'RE DISRESPECTING YOUR TEAMMATES! I'M ORDERING YOU TO GET BACK TO WORK – RIGHT NOW!'

'I HAVE TO LISTEN TO MY BODY! AND MY BODY IS TELLING ME THAT I'VE DONE MORE THAN ENOUGH WORK FOR ONE DAY!'

'DON'T YOU DARE GET INTO THE BACK OF THAT LIMO!'

'HEY, YOU COULD DO WITH MAYBE CHILLING OUT YOURSELF!'

'DON'T YOU DARE GET INTO THE BACK OF THAT LIMO!'

I climbed into the back of the limo.

I told him, 'I'LL SEE YOU AT THE MATCH NEXT SATURDAY!'

## 28  *In a Different League*

'I've had an idea for a prank!' Conor announced. 'And it's the best idea EVER!'

It was nearly midnight and we couldn't sleep for the sound of Peter snoring.

HOOOCCCKKK . . . ZZZUUUUUU!!!!!!

HOOOCCCKKK . . . ZZZUUUUUU!!!!!!

HOOOCCCKKK . . . ZZZUUUUUU!!!!!!

'Okay,' I asked, 'what's this prank?'

'It's brilliant,' he said. 'I have a roll of clingfilm in my drawer. We get up, then we go around to ALL the toilets in the school. We lift up the seat, we put a layer of clingfilm over the bowl, so that it acts as an invisible forcefield. Then we put the seat back down. And when people go for a pee . . .'

'It bounces off!' I said. 'Oh my God, Conor, that is pure genius!'

I sat up in my coffin and threw back my duvet.

'Okay,' I said, 'let's go.'

'Stay where you are!' Barry said. 'And I'm saying that as your agent!'

'But, Barry,' I said, 'this is an AMAZING idea! Think about it! No one will know WHY their pee is bending in the middle!'

'Do you not think it's a bit childish?' he said. 'A bit juvenile?'

'It's just a prank,' Conor said. 'Darce loves my pranks – except that time when I put a bag full of fish guts on the Wexford Wanderers' team bus.'

'Darce is an Ireland rugby international now,' Barry told him. 'He's got a lot more to lose than you do.'

'Like what?'

'His brand identity.'

'His *what*?'

'Do you think Brian O'Driscoll and Ronan O'Gara are putting clingfilm over toilet bowls tonight?'

'I don't know,' Conor said. 'Probably.'

'No, they're not,' Barry insisted. 'They're in bed, thinking about the match on Saturday. Which what Darce should be doing.'

He had a point. I lay back down and pulled the

duvet over me again. I tried to think about Scotland.

'Hey, Darce,' Conor said then. 'Can you do me a favour?'

'Yeah,' I said. 'As long as it's not a prank.'

'It's not a prank,' he said. 'My next-door neighbour in Wexford is a big fan of yours. He was wondering would you autograph a rugby ball for him?'

'Yeah,' I said. 'No problem at all.'

'Great,' Conor said, feeling around on the floor for it, 'it's under my bed here somewhere. Ah, there it is.'

'WAIT!' Barry shouted, then he switched on his bedside light. 'DON'T SIGN THAT!'

'Why not?' I asked.

'Because it's not Official Gordon D'Arcy Merchandise.'

'It's for his next-door neighbour,' I told him.

'As your agent,' he said, 'I'm telling you not to put your signature on anything that isn't Official Gordon D'Arcy Merchandise.'

'What exactly *is* Official Gordon D'Arcy Merchandise?' I asked.

'It'll be arriving tomorrow,' he said. 'A range of exciting products – t-shirts, mobile-phone covers, posters, mugs, toothbrushes – all with your image on them . . .'

'Wow!'

'And this slogan I've come up with . . .'

'What slogan?'

'Gordon D'Arcy – Total Legend!'

'I'm sorry, Conor,' I said. 'Maybe this neighbour of yours could buy a Gordon D'Arcy – Total Legend! t-shirt and I'll sign that for him instead?'

'That's a great idea,' Barry said. 'Now, can we PLEASE get some sleep.'

'I *can't* sleep,' I said. 'Not with that noise.'

HOOOCCCKKK . . . ZZZUUUUUU!!!!!!
HOOOCCCKKK . . . ZZZUUUUUU!!!!!!
HOOOCCCKKK . . . ZZZUUUUUU!!!!!!

'You know, you're absolutely right,' Barry said, throwing back his own covers, then jumping down from the top bunk. He put on his dressing gown and his slippers and he left the dorm.

As soon as he was gone, Conor said, 'You're not the same Godron D'Arcy you used to be.'

'What do you mean by that?' I asked.

'Since you became famous. You're different.'

'Is this because I don't want to do one of your stupid pranks? You heard what Barry said, Conor, it could hurt my brand identity.'

'It's not that.'

'Is it because I refused to sign that ball for your neighbour?'

'It's everything. You're not the Gordon D'Arcy you were a few months ago.'

'I know. I'm the Gordon D'Arcy who plays rugby for Ireland. I'm in a different league now. And I'm sorry if you can't handle that, Conor.'

'What is that supposed to mean?'

'Barry thinks you're jealous of my success. And I'm beginning to think he might be right.'

A second or two later, Barry reappeared. With him were four Sixth Year prefects.

'It's this guy here,' Barry told them, pointing at Peter. 'It goes on like that all night long.'

HOOOCCCKKK ... ZZZUUUUUU!!!!!!
HOOOCCCKKK ... ZZZUUUUUU!!!!!!
HOOOCCCKKK ... ZZZUUUUUU!!!!!!

The boys shook Peter awake. He opened his eyes, but he must have thought he was still dreaming.

'Who are you?' he said, reaching for his glasses. 'What's going on?'

'You're moving to another room,' Barry told him.

The prefects started removing his possessions from his locker and putting them into black bin-liners.

'Why are you moving him?' Conor asked.

'Because Gordon has a big match on Saturday,' Barry said, 'and he needs his sleep. What's he going to tell Ryle Nugent? "Yeah, I dropped the ball because I haven't slept all week on account of the fact that I share a bedroom with a boy who snores like a rhinoceros"? That can't happen.'

Peter was out of the bed now and the prefects were hustling him out of the room.

'Darce, stop them!' Conor pleaded with me. 'Peter's your friend, Darce!'

But all I could say was: 'Barry's right, Conor. I do need my sleep.'

'Well, if Peter's gone,' Conor said, climbing out of bed, 'then I'm gone, too.'

He started to pack up all of his possessions.

'Good riddance,' Barry said, 'to bad rubbish.'

## 29  *A Brand-New Gordon*

Conor and Peter made a big point of ignoring me the following day. As I walked past them on my way to the cafeteria, they both turned their heads so that they wouldn't have to say hello to me

I felt bad. But Barry was right. If I was going to be on top of my game, I really DID need my sleep. And, as Barry said, if I'd signed that ball for Conor's neighbour, maybe he would have sold it on eBay for a small fortune and kept the money for himself.

No, the problem, as I saw it, was that Conor and Peter were struggling to come to terms with my new status as a sporting superstar. And, as Barry said, that was *their* issue – not mine!

I didn't mind that they weren't speaking to me. Since I'd become famous, I had more friends than I knew what to do with. They literally fought each other for the honour of sitting beside me in class.

I didn't need Conor and Peter dragging me down to their level. Especially that morning, because I had just received some very exciting news. The Official Gordon D'Arcy – Total Legend! Merchandise had arrived. The mugs. The t-shirts. The posters. The mobile-phone covers. The toothbrushes.

Barry had set up a table for me in the cafeteria. He was going to sell the merchandise and I was going to sign it.

'Darce,' he told me excitedly, 'there's already a queue out the door!'

He wasn't exaggerating. When I reached the cafeteria, nearly every boy in the school was standing in line, waiting to buy something with my signature on it.

I sat down and started to sign everything that was put in front of me – provided it was Official Gordon D'Arcy Merchandise, of course.

And Barry made sure that it was.

'I'm a big, big fan,' one student told me. 'I'm looking forward to seeing what you do against Scotland.'

'Thanks,' I said. 'As long as the other lads give me plenty of the ball.'

'PLEASE DON'T SPEAK TO MY CLIENT!' Barry shouted at the queue of people. 'HE'S

SAVING HIS ENERGY FOR SATURDAY! IF YOU WISH TO ENGAGE WITH HIM, YOU CAN SIGN UP FOR THE GORDON D'ARCY RUGBY SCHOOL OF EXCELLENCE DURING THE EASTER HOLIDAYS! AND PLEASE TRY TO HAVE THE EXACT CHANGE FOR YOUR OFFICIAL MERCHANDISE BECAUSE IT KEEPS THE QUEUE MOVING ALONG!'

All of a sudden, there was a loud chorus of gasps in the cafeteria. I was in the middle of signing a t-shirt when I suddenly felt the weight of someone staring at me.

I looked up.

It was Aoife.

She GLOWERED at me.

'Where were you on Friday night?' she asked.

I could hear all the other boys going, 'Whooooaaa!!!'

Barry started looking over her shoulder for one of the teachers.

'Sorry, can we remove this girl, please?' he asked. 'This is supposed to be a school for boys – how can she just march in here like this?'

'I asked you a question,' Aoife said. 'You promised to do a coaching session with us. You told me you'd be there.'

'I, er, had a lot of homework to do,' I lied.

She threw a newspaper down on the table in front of me. I saw a photograph of myself on the red carpet at the James Bond premiere.

'Homework, huh?' she said.

'Look, the thing is,' I tried to explain, 'I promised to do that BEFORE I realized just how big I'd become.'

'Excuse me?'

'What I'm trying to say, Aoife, is that I'm in a different league now. Look, if you want me to coach your team, you *could* always sign up for the Gordon D'Arcy Rugby School of Excellence.'

'The Gordon D'Arcy Rugby School of Excellence? Are you *actually* serious?'

'Yeah,' I said, flicking my thumb in Barry's direction. 'Talk to my agent.'

But Aoife didn't talk to my agent. She just looked at me, shook her head and said, 'You might be a great rugby player, Gordon D'Arcy, but you are NOT a very nice person.'

She dropped something onto the table in front of me. I looked down. It was the Ireland jersey I'd given to her to show her parents. Except now it was rolled into a ball. And then she stormed out.

The bell rang for the end of lunchtime.

Barry shouted, 'APOLOGIES TO EVERYONE WHO DIDN'T GET THEIR OFFICIAL GORDON D'ARCY MERCHANDISE TODAY! WE WILL BE BACK HERE AT THE SAME TIME TOMORROW!'

I stood up from the table. My hand was sore from all the signatures I'd performed. I had Double Geography next, but I decided not to bother going. Instead, I told Barry that I was going to head back to the dorm to sleep for the afternoon.

'I think that's an EXCELLENT idea,' he said.

I was on my way back to the room when I bumped into Mr Murray.

'Gordon,' he said, 'how's it going?'

'All good,' I said. 'I'm looking forward to the Scotland match on Saturday.'

'As am I,' he said. 'I got tickets.'

'Would you be interested in wearing a Gordon D'Arcy – Total Legend! t-shirt? I could probably get you some kind of discount.'

He looked at me like he thought I was mad.

'Thank you,' he said, 'but I'll probably wear my Ireland jersey, like I usually do. Gordon, can I give you some advice?'

'Er, yeah,' I said. 'I was going to take a nap, but I've got a minute or two.'

'Look, I can't help but notice that there's been a change in attitude towards you since the match in Paris. And I can't help but notice that there's been a change in *your* attitude as well.'

'Mine?'

'All I'm saying is, Gordon, this whole celebrity thing you're enjoying right now, it's not real. In a few weeks' time, it will have passed on to someone else. Just don't lose sight of the things that are important.'

That's what he *said*. But all I could hear was: 'Blah, blah, blah, blah, blah, blah, blah.'

# 30  *The Green-Haired Monster*

It was the day before we played Scotland. We were leaving Double Chemistry when Barry told me that he'd arranged an interview for me.

'An interview?' I said. 'With who?'

'Have you ever heard of the *Sunday Bugle*?' he asked.

'Yeah,' I told him, 'that's the paper my dad buys!'

'Well, you're going to be in it this Sunday! Their showbiz correspondent is waiting for you outside in the car park. And she's brought a photographer with her.'

'Why?'

'Because you're hot right now. The world is interested in hearing what you have to say.'

'What I mean is, maybe I shouldn't do any interviews until *after* the match tomorrow?'

'Hey, all I'm trying to do is build up your brand so we can maximize your earning potential. But if you're not interested in being a celebrity, I can always tell her that the interview is off.'

'No, please don't,' I said, 'I'll do it.'

'Fine,' he said. 'But don't tell anyone and try not to let anyone see you doing it because I haven't cleared it with the school.'

'So what kind of questions is she going to ask me?' I wondered.

'Don't worry,' Barry said. 'Just be yourself, okay?'

'Okay.'

'But don't tell her you're from Wexford.'

'What? Why not?'

'I'm just not sure if Wexford fits with the image I'm trying to create for you right now.'

'But I'm PROUD to be from Wexford!'

'I'd keep that to yourself as well. You see, Gordon, superstars come from big cities – they don't come from little villages in the middle of nowhere. Let's be honest, Wexford is a pimple on the bum of Ireland.'

'I see it more as a beauty spot on the bum of Ireland.'

'Either way, if she asks you where you're from, change the subject, okay?'

'Okay.'

'And don't be afraid to talk yourself up. No modesty, right?'

'Right.'

'But, other than bigging yourself up and denying that you're from Wexford, just be yourself.'

We went outside. There was a young woman waiting for us in the car park. Next to her was a large man with FIVE cameras dangling from his neck.

'Hi,' the woman said, offering me her hand, 'I'm Hazel Greene, Showbiz Correspondent with the *Sunday Bugle*.'

'Gordon D'Arcy,' I said, shaking her hand.

She laughed. 'Yeah,' she said, 'like the whole country doesn't know who you are? This is Steve, the photographer. Do you mind if we do the pictures *while* we talk?'

'Er, not at all,' I said.

'I've got this idea,' Steve said, 'for the photographs. I was going to ask you to rub some of this into your hair.'

He produced a little plastic tub.

'What is it?' I asked.

'It's green hair dye,' he said.

'Brilliant!' Barry said. 'Showing your commitment to Ireland by having green hair! You see, *this* is the kind of image I want for you, Darce!'

So I agreed to do it. I took the tub from Steve.
I dipped my fingers into the tub – it felt like cold
slime – and I rubbed it into my hair.

'Oh, it looks FANTASTIC!' Hazel said.

'It really suits you,' Barry agreed. 'As a matter of
fact, I think you should keep it like that for the
match tomorrow.'

Steve got me to hold a rugby ball and smile for
the camera while Hazel fired questions at me.

'I'm interested in finding out about you,' she said.

'Tell me something about you that NOBODY knows.'

'Well,' I said, 'I've got one brother and two sisters –'

'BORING!' she shouted.

'What?' I said.

'Tell me something INTERESTING about you. For instance, how has your life changed since you became a famous rugby player?'

'It hasn't changed that much really.'

I could see that Barry was shaking his head. This clearly wasn't doing much for my brand identity.

'Oh, enough with the false modesty!' Hazel said. 'A month ago, you were a nobody! People heard your name and said, "Gordon who?" Now, you're the star player on the IRELAND RUGBY TEAM! You can't tell me that people don't look at you differently.'

'Well, I suppose they do,' I agreed.

'How do they look at you now?'

'I don't know. Differently?'

'In awe? Can I put down, in awe?'

'Er, I suppose you *could* say awe, yeah.'

She scribbled something in her notebook.

'What do you say to those people who say you're nothing more than a flash in the pan?' she asked.

'Which people?' I said.

'Oh, they're out there, don't you worry about that. As soon as you become successful, there are some people who can't wait to see you fail. You're not a flash in the pan, are you?'

'No, definitely not.'

'Are you the best young Irish player to come along for fifty years?'

'What?'

'Because that's what *other* people are saying about you. What do you say? Do you agree with them?'

I looked at Barry and he nodded.

'Yeah, I suppose so,' I said. 'One of the best, definitely.'

'Can I quote you as saying that? The best young Irish player to come along for fifty years?'

'Er, okay.'

'Do you think you're better than Ronan O'Gara, then?'

'Er . . . maybe?'

'He means *definitely*,' Barry said.

'Do you think you're better than Brian O'Driscoll?' she asked.

'Er . . .' I said.

'That sounds like another yes to me. Do you think you're better than Rob Kearney?'

'Er . . .'

'I'll just write yes again.'

She thanked me for the interview and photographs and then she and Steve left.

'Was that okay?' I asked Barry.

'Okay?' Barry said. 'It was great! You were just YOU! Or, rather, the YOU I want the world to think you are!'

We walked back to the dorm. It felt kind of empty now that Peter and Conor had moved out to a room further down the corridor. But Barry said that superstars need their space.

I looked at myself in the mirror. My hair was exactly the same colour green as the jersey I'd be wearing against Scotland tomorrow. I really liked it.

'I think you're right,' I said. 'I'm not going to bother washing my hair before the match tomorrow.'

'The fans are going to LOVE it!' Barry assured me. 'By the way, I've got a present for you.'

He reached into his locker and took out a cardboard shoebox, which he handed to me.

'What is it?' I asked.

'Open it,' he said.

I lifted the lid. Inside was the most magnificent pair of rugby boots I had ever seen. They were gold in colour. Very shiny gold.

In white lettering, across the heel of one boot, was the word:

'TOTAL.'

And across the other one, it said:

'LEGEND.'

I sat down on my study chair and put them on. They were the perfect fit.

'I love them,' I said. 'But they're not too –'

'What?'

'– blingy, are they?'

'Blingy is good!' Barry replied. 'You want to stand out, don't you?'

'I suppose so.'

Barry had an idea then.

'Hey,' he said, 'let's phone out for a pizza.'

'A pizza?' I said.

'They'll deliver to the school, won't they?' he said.

'It's just, I'm pretty sure that's not the kind of thing I should be eating the night before a big match.'

'Gordon, *relax*!' he said. 'It's only Scotland!'

# 31 *Only Scotland*

It was very odd. I was much more relaxed this time. There were none of the nerves that I'd felt before the match in Paris. My heart wasn't even beating fast as I sat in the dressing room to hear Warren give us our pre-match talk.

'Some people think Scotland are an easy team to beat,' he said. 'Well, let me tell you something, they're not. And we'd be fools to underestimate them. Because I'll tell you something about this Scottish team. No team works harder in training. They know they're not as good as us, which is why they train harder than any other team in the Six Nations. There's an old saying, guys – hard work beats talent when talent doesn't work hard!'

For a split-second, I could have sworn that he looked at me when he said that.

'They've come here today to beat us. And beat us they will, unless we're at the top of our game.'

I felt a yawn coming on. I decided to just go with it.

Warren stared at me. 'You tired, Gordon?' he asked.

'No,' I told him. 'I'm just unbelievably relaxed.'

He shook his head like he was disappointed. I sensed he was still annoyed with me for walking out on training that day. But I had done enough. As Barry said, pain is the body's way of telling you to give up and call it a day.

'I hope you're ready for this,' he said. 'I'm trusting you.'

'I've got this, Warren,' I said confidently.

I noticed two or three of my teammates rolling their eyes. They clearly weren't happy with me for leaving training either. Judging by the looks they were giving me, one or two of them were pretty jealous of my new-look hair – not to mention my boots.

'Where did you get those?' Paulie asked me.

'They were a present,' I told him, 'from my agent. I don't know if you've ever heard of Flash Barry Considine?'

'Er, no, I haven't.'

'I can give you his card if you want.'

'You're grand, thanks.'

'If you change your mind, let me know. He was the one who gave me the boots. I don't know if you can read it, but it says TOTAL on one and LEGEND on the other.'

'I can see that,' he said.

'I wonder will the TV cameras pick up on them?'

'Oh, I'm sure they will.'

'That's good. I want people at home to see them.'

'The thing is, Gordon, you have to be very, very good to get away with a pair of boots like that.'

But I WAS very, very good. Or so I thought.

Soon, it was time to go out and play. We left the dressing room, then we lined up in the tunnel next to the Scotland team. I could see some of the Scottish players checking out my hair and my boots and smiling. And I thought, Well, at least someone appreciates a showman around here!

A minute or so later, we got the signal and we walked out onto the pitch. I had been to matches in the Aviva Stadium with Dad. The atmosphere was always incredible. But down on the pitch, the noise of the crowd sounded even more deafening.

The Stade de France was a bigger stadium, but

there is nothing like playing in front of your home supporters – especially for the first time. As I warmed up, I heard the crowd chant, 'D'Arcy! D'Arcy! D'Arcy!' and I suddenly felt very proud of how far I'd come.

We lined up for the national anthems. While the band played 'Amhrán na bhFiann', I squinted into the West Stand and tried to pick out Mum and Dad, Ian, Shona and Megan. I couldn't see them, but I spotted one or two fans who were holding up a 'Gordon D'Arcy – Total Legend!' banner. I gave them a big thumbs-up.

Beside me, Paulie said, 'Focus, Gordon!'

I thought to myself, What's *his* problem? because he was a bit cranky with me in the dressing room as well.

The anthems ended. BOD walked up to me as I was doing a few final stretches.

'So what's with the hair?' he asked.

'Cool, huh?' I said.

'It's a bit "look at me", isn't it?'

'Hey, chill out, will you?'

'Chill out? We're about to play a match! We shouldn't *be* chilled out!'

'It's only Scotland.'

251

'Darce, you heard what the coach said, you've got to respect every opponent equally.'

'I know, but it's not like they're France, right?'

He just shook his head in a disappointed way and walked off.

Scotland kicked off.

Gordon Ross, the Scottish outhalf, put the ball high in the air. And once again — just as it happened against France — it was mine to claim.

I watched the ball dropping towards me, faster this time.

Now, though, I was FULLY aware of the crowd.

I thought to myself, Okay, this shouldn't be too hard. I wonder can the crowd see what's written on my boots?

And then suddenly —

Oh, no!

I dropped the ball.

And half a second after that . . .

BAAANNNGGG!!!

Graeme Morrison, the big Scottish centre, tackled me. I felt like I'd been run over by a bus.

Scotland had stolen the ball. I was lying on the

252

ground, birds twittering around my head. I looked up, waiting for one of my teammates to put out a hand to help me up. But no one did.

They just ignored me.

Things went from bad to worse after that. Every time someone played a pass to me, I knocked the ball on . . .

Or it went through my hands . . .

Or I was too far ahead of the ball when it arrived . . .

Or too far behind it . . .

And soon, every time I got my hands on the ball, the crowd groaned in one voice. It was:

'Uuunnnhhh!!!'

Or it was:

'Aaahhhhhhhhh!!!!!!'

Or it was:

'Eeerrrggghhh!!!'

Because they *expected* me to do something wrong. And I did. Every single time. Until my teammates stopped passing it to me altogether.

And something else happened, too. I was EX-HAUSTED. I couldn't even keep up with the play.

'How long until half-time?' I asked the referee.

He looked at me like I was from another planet.

'We've only been playing for ten minutes!' he said.

*Ten minutes?*

I was thinking, how could I be this tired already? I was fine against France. Could it have something to do with the sixteen-inch pizza I ate last night? Or the bucket of nachos smothered in cheese that I ate while watching the Bond film? Or the ten sausages and mountain of beans I'd eaten for breakfast every single morning since the match against France?

The game passed me by. I sleepwalked my way through the first half, wishing I was somewhere else.

Eventually, the half-time whistle blew. I didn't even know the score. I was so focused on how badly *I* was playing that I had no idea we were losing by 14–3.

And there was no doubt who the rest of the team blamed. None of them could even look at me.

'Where's the hunger I saw against France two weeks ago?' Warren asked. He was talking to the entire team, but I could tell that he was staring at my boots. 'It's like you did something great in Paris and you started to believe your own hype! You've forgotten that this is supposed to be hard work!'

Warren looked directly at me then. 'You've got ten minutes,' he said, 'to save your Ireland career.'

That should have made me spur into action and

save the day, but I was so tired when the second half started, I could have lain down and fallen asleep there on the pitch with the match going on around me.

When I tried to run, my boots of gold felt like boots of lead.

And then it started to rain. A real downpour. And something very, very embarrassing happened. During a break in the play, I ran my hand through my hair and I noticed that my fingers . . .

. . . were green!

The dye was washing out of my hair. Graeme Morrison, the Scottish centre, laughed when he saw my face.

'Hey, son,' he said, 'your roots are showing!'

The dye was running down my forehead and down my cheeks in great big rivers of green. I was distracted by it. I had to keep wiping it out of my eyes.

A moment later, I picked up a loose ball and decided to throw a miss-pass to Rob Kearney. I was playing so badly that I felt I had to do something special to get the crowd off my back. I threw a long, looping pass over the head of BOD to Rob. But the problem was I hadn't practised it properly that day in Greystones. The ball was never going to find him. I knew from the moment it left my hands that I hadn't put enough pace on it.

It seemed to travel in slow motion.

And I watched in horror as Kenny Logan, the Scottish wing, intercepted it and ran on to score a try.

Ireland were now losing 21–3.

Even through eyes full of green dye, I could see the board with the number twelve on it being held up on the sideline.

The match was over for me.

'Substitute for Ireland,' the stadium announcer said. 'Gordon D'Arcy is being replaced by Kevin Maggs!'

The crowd cheered, happy that I was being put out of my misery – and out of harm's way, where I couldn't cost us any more points.

I walked off the field, feeling like every set of eyes in that stadium was fixed on me.

Warren patted me on the back. 'Bad luck,' he said. 'You win some, you lose some.'

My stomach was sick with the feeling that I'd let everyone down. I heard people in the crowd saying:

'He just got lucky in Paris!'

And:

'Golden boots? The nerve of the lad!'

And:

'That's the last we'll be seeing of HIM in an Ireland jersey!'

I walked into the tunnel. And that's when I saw him there, waiting for me . . .

My dad.

I burst into tears. He wrapped his arms around me. He didn't seem to mind at all that his clothes were getting covered in green dye.

'I blew it!' I sobbed. 'I don't know what happened, Dad! The whole thing just went to my head!'

Dad chuckled. 'You look like Shrek!' he said.

'How can you make jokes?' I asked.

'Because it's not the end of the world, Gordon. You're so young. And you've got so many things still to learn.'

'I had it all and I threw it away.'

'One day you'll look back on this experience and you'll realize it was the best thing that ever happened to you.'

I didn't see how that was possible. There was no coming back from this. It didn't matter how well I'd played in Paris. This is how I would be remembered. A failure in golden boots with a big pizza belly and green dye all over his face. I didn't think it was possible to feel any worse.

But then, I hadn't seen the following day's *Sunday Bugle* yet.

## 32  *Lonely at the Top*

Mum and Dad drove me back to Clongowes on Sunday night, after spending the night at home in Wexford. For the first time, I wasn't excited to be going back to school.

We parked outside the school building and they asked me how I was feeling. I was sitting on my own in the back of the car.

'Scared,' I said. 'Nervous.'

They both nodded their heads like they understood.

'Look,' Dad said, 'I'm not going to pretend that it's going to be easy for you going back to school after what happened yesterday. But everyone makes mistakes, Gordon. There's nothing special about you in that regard. It's how we come back from those mistakes that defines us as people. Do you understand?'

I said I did, even though I probably didn't.

'What if they've all read the *Sunday Bugle*?' I asked.

Mum laughed. 'You really talked yourself up to that reporter,' she said, 'didn't you?'

My toes curled when I thought about some of the things that had appeared in the newspaper, some of which I hadn't even said:

'I'm the best Irish player of all time!'

'They'll still be talking about my performance against France in a thousand years' time!'

'I'm better than Brian O'Driscoll, Ronan O'Gara and Rob Kearney rolled into one!'

What made the whole Scotland failure even more embarrassing was that as soon as I left the field, Ireland staged an heroic comeback. And it was those three exact players – BOD, Rob and ROG – who scored the tries as Ireland went on to win 24–21.

I was cringing inside.

'You just got carried away,' Mum said. 'Like you used to when you were a little boy. Do you remember the time you put on that picnic for us?'

I couldn't help but laugh.

'Stop,' I said. 'You're making me feel better, and I don't deserve to feel better.'

'There's no badness in you, Gordon,' she told me. 'You just get carried away sometimes. But we love you all the more for that.'

I leaned forward between the seats and I gave them both a hug.

'It's just two more days,' Dad reminded me. Tuesday was the start of the Easter holidays. 'By the time everyone comes back from their Easter break, this will all be old news.'

Slowly, I got out of the car. As I walked towards the school building, I thought about what Dad had said. I took a deep breath, then I pushed open the door and walked inside.

The lobby was filled with the loud, excited chatter of boys returning to school after spending the weekend at home. When they saw me, every conversation seemed to stop dead. Suddenly, there was just perfect silence. A hundred kids – maybe even more – stopped what they were doing and just stared at me like they were seeing a ghost.

Then one of the Sixth Years shouted, 'Where's your golden boots, Darce?'

Everyone laughed.

Another older boy said to me, 'I saw the interview in the *Sunday Bugle*! The best Irish player of the last fifty years? You're a joke!'

I looked across the lobby and I saw Conor and Peter. They were looking at me with sad faces, no hint of a smile. When I waved to them, they both turned away from me. I deserved it. I deserved every bit of it and more.

I made my way through the crowd in the direction of the dormitories. In the corridor, I noticed that someone had pinned one of my Official Merchandise posters to the noticeboard. But they'd crossed out the word 'Legend' and replaced it with 'Loser'.

I didn't even bother taking it down. I just thought, Let them get it out of their systems. Hopefully, Dad was right – they'll have forgotten about it in a week or two.

I went to my dorm. Barry was in there. Everything from his wardrobe and locker was spread out on the bed and he was stuffing it all into a bag.

'You're moving out,' I said – it was more of an observation than a question.

'Yes, I am,' he said. 'There's a guy three doors down who's just been selected to play tennis at Junior Wimbledon!'

'And let me guess,' I said. '*You're* going to be his agent?'

'He needs the kind of guidance that only Barry Considine – Agent to the Stars can offer!'

'Are you going to get him to do an interview with the *Sunday Bugle*? Get your reporter friend to put all sorts of words in his mouth?'

Barry stopped packing his bags.

'I'm sort of picking up on a vibe here that you're upset,' he said.

'Of course I'm upset,' I told him. 'I had it all, Barry. And now I've lost everything. My rugby career. My friends . . .'

'I hate to break it to you, but you've lost quite a bit of money as well.'

'What are you talking about?'

'Well, you owe me eighty quid for the taxi we took back to school after the movie premiere. And five hundred quid for the limo that took you to training that day.'

'But the limo was *your* idea!'

'*The client is responsible for ALL transportation costs.* It's in your contract.'

'I didn't sign any contract.'

'Yeah, I signed it for you. I told you I was good at doing other people's handwriting, didn't I?'

He continued packing.

'What about all the money from the Official Gordon D'Arcy Merchandise we sold?' I asked him.

'That's not going to last long,' he said, 'especially at the rate that people are coming to me asking for refunds.'

'I don't believe this!'

'Look, I'll do a deal with you. I've been left with a lot of Official Gordon D'Arcy Merchandise that no one is going to want now that you're a big, fat failure. No offence.'

'What do you mean *no offence*? How could I *not* be offended by that?'

'What I *could* do is send all of the unsold merchandise back to the manufacturers and get them to change the slogan to Steven Varsey – Total Legend!'

'Who's Steven Varsey?'

'He's the guy who's going to be playing at Junior Wimbledon. He is *so* talented. He reminds me a lot of you – in the early days.'

Barry finished packing his bags, then he walked to the door. Before he left, he looked back at me.

'I told you it was a small window of opportunity,' he said. 'No one stays on top forever – not even the greats.'

'It was only three weeks,' I said.

'Hey,' he said, 'some people don't even get that! Do you want to punch me in the stomach?'

'Yes,' I said, 'I do! I really, really do, Barry – but I'm working really hard here to try to stop myself!'

'Please yourself,' he said. 'See you round, Darce.'

And then he was gone, leaving me all alone in that big, four-bed dormitory. I switched off the light and cried myself to sleep.

# 33  *The Laws of Gravity*

That was how Monday and Tuesday went. People laughed when they saw me coming in the hallway. Or they shouted horrible – and horribly true – comments at me.

I grit my teeth and made it through those days, just waiting until I could return to Wexford for two whole weeks.

I was sitting in Double Physics, the last class before we broke for the holidays. Mr McManus was talking about gravity.

'Gravity,' he said, 'is the natural force that causes things to fall towards the Earth. It's the law that says that what goes up must also come down again. Can anyone give an example that proves the law of gravity?'

Someone at the back of the class shouted:

'Gordon D'Arcy!'

That drew huge laughter in the class. One week ago, everyone in this school was proud of me, pushing to get to sit next to me. Now, I was the punchline to a joke.

I was sitting at the back of the class and all I could see were sets of shoulders going up and down as my classmates laughed at me. All except two. Conor and Peter didn't laugh. I saw them exchange a look.

'That's not a very kind thing to say,' Mr McManus said. 'Although it *is* also true. Gordon D'Arcy is an EXCELLENT example of something that went up but then was forced to come back down to Earth again.'

On the blackboard, he drew a long arrow pointing upwards, then beside it a second arrow pointing downwards, while I prayed for the bell to end my misery.

It finally rang. The day was over, and so was the week.

As we were leaving the class, I caught up with Conor and Peter.

'Can I talk to you?' I asked.

Conor shrugged. 'It's a free country,' he said.

He was still hurt. They were both still hurt.

'I wanted to apologize,' I said. 'It just went to my

head and I acted like a complete eejit. Not only that but I treated you in a way that no one should ever treat their friends. Peter, I'm sorry I got you thrown out of the dorm. And, Conor, I'm sorry I refused to sign your rugby ball.'

They both nodded but didn't say anything.

'I know you're both still upset,' I said, 'and probably still angry about the way I behaved. And I don't really know how to apologize for something like this, other than to say I'm really, really sorry – and I hope one day you'll give me the chance to make it up to you both.'

I could feel my eyes filling up with tears. I didn't want to cry in school. I was a big enough laughing stock as it was. So I told them to enjoy the holidays and I took off out of there without looking back.

I went outside and waited for Mum and Dad to collect me in the car.

In the distance, on the rugby field, I could see the girls from St Bridget's training. I owed them an apology, too – especially Aoife. But I just didn't have the strength in me at that moment.

Suddenly, a man's voice behind me said, 'Gordon?'

I turned around. It was Mr Murray.

'How are you?' he asked.

'Not great,' I told him. 'Not great at all.'

'That's kind of understandable,' he said, 'after what you've been through. It's bad enough to have something like that happen to you without it happening in front of the entire country.'

'In front of the entire world,' I reminded him. 'The Six Nations is watched in one hundred and forty countries.'

Mr Murray laughed. I didn't, though.

'You're clearly not ready to look on the bright side, then,' he said.

'What bright side?' I wondered.

'Gordon, this all happened for you at a very young age. When you get older, you'll develop a better perspective on things like this.'

'I don't know what that means.'

'It means that nobody died, Gordon. It means that you've lived to fight another day. And my prediction is that one day, in the not-too-distant future, you're going to look back on these past few weeks and you're going to say it was the best thing that could have happened to you.'

'What? How can you say that? Everyone is laughing at me.'

'Gordon, you're a great rugby player. That hasn't changed. And you're going to get another chance.'

'Do you really think so?'

'I do. And the second time around, you'll be ready for it. You'll appreciate it more because you've had this experience. And because you've learned a valuable lesson, Gordon. Nothing good in life comes without hard work.'

I thought to myself, Where did I hear that before? Someone in the distant past had told me the exact same thing, but in that moment, I couldn't remember who had said it.

I watched Dad's car pull up in front of me.

'Think about what I said,' Mr Murray told me. 'And try to enjoy the break.'

## 34  *A Spark of Inspiration*

I tried my best to remember what Mr Murray had told me, but I was miserable. I spent most of the week at home moping around in my bedroom.

Everyone in the family made an effort to get me to snap out of the bad mood I was in.

On Thursday afternoon, I was watching TV in my room. Megan threw little stones up at my bedroom window. I looked out.

She shouted up at me, 'Do you want to play hopscotch?'

I noticed that she'd drawn little numbered boxes on the road in front of the house. One to ten.

'No, thanks, Megan,' I said. 'Maybe tomorrow.'

I wasn't in the mood for games of any kind – even hopscotch. Knowing me, I'd probably mess it up anyway. I'd drop the chalk or fall flat on my face!

On Friday, it was Shona's turn to try to get me to snap out of it.

'I'm going into town,' she said, 'if you want to come with me? I'll buy you a milkshake!'

'I think I'll stay here, Shona,' I said. 'I'm, er, not ready to face the world yet.'

On Sunday, Ian had a go. He knocked on my bedroom door, then he stuck his head around it.

'Are you coming downstairs,' he asked, 'to watch the match?'

'What match?' I asked.

Ian laughed. 'What match?' he said. 'Ireland are playing Italy! In the Six Nations!'

I had totally forgotten that Ireland had a game today.

'Come on,' he said, 'me and Dad are going to watch it.'

But I couldn't. It would be too painful.

'I might give it a miss,' I said, 'if it's all the same to you.'

Ian nodded, then he walked over and sat down on my bed.

'Looking back,' he said, 'do you know what I loved most about rugby?'

'Scoring tries?' I said.

'No, not scoring tries.'

'The crowd singing 'Mill 'Em', Darce?'

'No – although I *did* enjoy that. No, the thing I loved most about rugby was the lessons it taught me about life.'

'What lessons?'

'It taught me how to win and how to lose. That's the thing about playing sport, Gordon – any sport. You're going to experience the highest highs and you're going to experience the lowest lows.'

'Did you ever feel like this after playing badly?'

'Every single time. But it's like life, Gordon. Sometimes you have a bad day. But guess what? There's a brand-new one starting tomorrow. And another one after that. If you change your mind, we'll be downstairs.'

I thought about what Ian had said. But I wasn't just upset about a rugby match. I was sad about the way I'd treated my friends. I was thinking about Conor and Peter and all the fun they were probably having on their Easter break. Although Peter was probably mostly in the library, studying.

The point was that I missed them and I was angry with myself for pushing them away.

Downstairs, I heard Dad and Ian cheering and I knew that Ireland were winning. They were winning WITHOUT ME! I covered my ears with my

pillow and tried to block out the sound of their happiness.

Later on, Mum called me for Sunday dinner. I shouted down the stairs that I wasn't hungry. But she told me that I had to eat – and from the way she said it, it didn't sound like I had any choice in the matter.

So I left my room and I went downstairs.

Dad and Ian were talking excitedly about a try that Ireland had scored. They stopped when I walked into the kitchen.

'Did Ireland win?' I asked.

'Er, yeah,' Ian answered, 'they did.'

'How did they play?'

'Just okay,' Dad said. 'I really think they missed you, though.'

I knew he was trying to spare my feelings.

'What score did they win by?' I asked.

'It was, em, 84–0 in the end,' Ian said.

Yes, they'd OBVIOUSLY missed me!

'How did Kevin Maggs play?' I asked. Kevin was the player who'd replaced me. 'Tell me the truth.'

'He played kind of well,' Ian admitted. 'He scored four tries.'

'Five,' Dad corrected.

'Five,' Ian said. 'I forgot about the last one.'

'Dinner will be on the table in two minutes!' Mum said. 'Go and wash your hands, all of you!'

'Honestly, Mum, I'm not really hungry,' I said.

But Dad told me to sit down at the table.

'Your mother has worked hard all afternoon to make a lovely Sunday dinner for us,' he said.

And at that exact moment, Mum opened the oven. And maybe it was Dad mentioning hard work, or maybe it was the smell of the roast potatoes, but I experienced a sudden flashback.

It can happen sometimes, when you're really, really sad, that you suddenly realize there's something you can do about it – and that, deep down, you knew all along what that something was.

'Dad,' I said, 'can I go back to Uncle Tim and Auntie Kathleen's farm?'

274

# 35 *Certain Qualities*

They laughed when they saw me standing at the front door. And I mean they REALLY laughed.

'Is it true what your father said on the phone?' Tim asked. 'You want to work on the farm for the week?'

Auntie Kathleen was standing behind him and so were my cousins, Anne, Clare, Mary, Teresa and Helena. They were all red in the face from laughing.

'I just want to remember what it feels like to work hard at something,' I told them.

'Gordon,' Teresa said, 'do you not remember what happened the last time you were here?'

'You were the WORST farmer in the world!' Mary reminded me. 'There's scarecrows out in that field would make better farmers than you, Gordon!'

'Do you remember the suit of armour he used to put on him every morning to collect the eggs?' said Anne.

'Do you remember him trying to catch Princess Layer?' said Clare.

'You're too soft for farm work!' Helena declared. 'And you're lazy as well – a bottle of your sweat would be worth millions!'

'It's different this time,' I said. 'I want to work. And I want to work hard.'

Again, they all fell about laughing. But then Uncle Tim saw that I wasn't laughing.

'By God,' he said, 'I think the lad might actually *mean* it!'

'I *do* mean it,' I promised him. 'So what do you think? Can I stay?'

'Of course you can stay!' said Auntie Kathleen, ushering me inside. 'You're welcome here any time!'

Dad was waiting outside in the car with the engine running. Uncle Tim waved to him and said, 'We'll take him for the night! I expect you'll probably have him wanting to come back home by dinnertime tomorrow, though!'

Clare took my bag and brought it to the spare bedroom where I'd slept the last time I'd stayed.

Auntie Kathleen sat me down at the kitchen table and put a mug of tea in front of me.

'Okay,' said Uncle Tim, sitting down beside me, 'if you're going to become a good farmer, you're going to need to develop certain qualities.'

'What kind of qualities?' I asked.

'Firstly, an appetite for hard work . . .'

'I've got that. Honestly.'

'. . . and early mornings.'

'I'm fine with that.'

'You'll need patience. You have to understand that things might not happen as easily as you expect them to happen. Or they might not happen at the speed you want them to happen. It's like when I asked you to put them chickens away that time – do you remember that?'

'Of course I do.'

'And you gave up, didn't you? Because it was too hard.'

'I won't this time. I swear.'

'Also, you need a sense of responsibility.'

'Okay, what's that exactly?'

'It's the knowledge that you are being relied upon to do certain jobs. And if you don't do those jobs properly, or if you cut corners, then there are consequences for others.'

'Right.'

He turned his head then and said, 'Helena, go and get Billy!'

Helena left the room.

'Billy?' I said, looking around me. 'Who's Billy?'

A second or two later, Helena returned. Cradled in her arms was a tiny, new-born lamb.

'This,' Uncle Tim said, 'is Billy.'

'What's wrong with him?' I asked.

'There's nothing at all wrong with him,' said Helena, 'except that his mother died giving birth to him – and now he's an orphan.'

My heart broke for that tiny little lamb. He looked so helpless and so scared.

'He's all alone in the world,' said Clare, 'which is why we call him Billy. It's short for Billy No Mates.'

'So who's going to look after him?' I asked.

'You are!' Helena said, putting him into my arms.

'Me?'

'That's right,' said Uncle Tim. 'You're going to bring him everywhere you go. When he's hungry, you're going to feed him milk from a bottle. When he's frightened, you're going to reassure him.'

'How do you reassure a lamb?' I asked.

'You'd be surprised by the things you know. The lesson here, Gordon, is that anything that's worth

278

having in life needs to be minded and nourished and not taken for granted. Do you know what I'm saying to you?'

I nodded.

'I won't let you down,' I told him.

'It's not me you'll be letting down,' he said. 'Billy is the one who's relying on you.'

I looked down at Billy, his head nestled in the crook of my arm.

'I won't let *you* down,' I told him. 'That's a promise.'

'And just to let you know,' Helena said, 'he wakes up VERY early in the morning.'

Helena wasn't lying. Billy woke up at three o'clock in the morning!

Yes, in the MORNING! That was a new one on me as well!

And for a little fella, he sure made a lot of noise.

'Ma-ha-ha-ha-ha-ha!' he went. He was lying beside me on the bed. 'Ma-ha-ha-ha-ha-ha!'

Uncle Tim had told me that was the noise he made when he was hungry.

I threw back the sheets, gathered him up in my

arms and carried him downstairs to the kitchen. I opened the fridge and took out the milk. I poured some into a saucepan then I heated it gently on the stove until it was warm. Then I poured it into a baby's bottle.

I sat down in Uncle Tim's chair, next to the fireplace, with Billy in my arms and he sucked

happily on the teat of the bottle while I talked softly to him.

'Take your time,' I whispered. 'No one's going to take it away from you. Just promise me that when you're finished you'll let me go back to sleep. Because I've got a big day ahead of me.'

When he was finished feeding, I took him back upstairs to bed. We both fell asleep quite quickly, but it seemed like only a few minutes later that Uncle Tim threw open the door of my bedroom and shouted:

'Wakey, wakey! Rise and shine!'

I didn't hestitate. I wanted to prove that I wasn't a quitter, that I could keep going, even when things got tough. I told myself that I was going to prove my worth to Uncle Tim and Auntie Kathleen, but I think I was really trying to prove it to myself, that I was capable of working hard and sticking with it.

I swung my legs out of the bed, picked up Billy and went down to the kitchen.

It gave me a huge thrill to see that I was up and out of bed before any of my cousins. They arrived down to breakfast one by one, looking bleary-eyed – and surprised to see me awake and dressed already, and eating a piece of toast.

Clare smiled at me and said, 'You're going to be asleep in about an hour!'

'We'll see about that,' I told her.

After breakfast, we all headed for the chicken shed to collect the eggs.

'Where's your oven gloves?' asked Mary.

'Don't need them,' I replied.

Into the shed we went. The smell was even worse than I remembered it. I felt my stomach lurch and I thought I might be sick at any moment. But I didn't let it show because I knew they'd be only too delighted to have a chance to call me soft again.

'The smell's not too bad at all,' I said, 'once you get used to it!'

I put Billy down on a little bed of straw, then I walked over to the first chicken coop. I could see an eye looking at me through a gap in the wood.

'Is that who I think it is?' I asked.

'It's Princess Layer,' said Uncle Tim. 'She's still going strong.'

I got ready to slip my hand into the gap at the bottom of the coop. In my head, I counted down from three.

Three . . .

Two . . .

One!

Then I slid my hand in and . . .

'OUCH!'

Princess Layer pecked me hard on the hand.

I winced.

'That really hurt,' I said.

Anne pushed me to one side. 'Remember,' she said, 'the hand is faster than the eye. I thought you were supposed to be good at rugby?'

'What does this have to do with rugby?' I wondered.

'Just imagine you're pulling the ball from a ruck.'

'I didn't think –'

'You didn't think girls were interested in rugby?'

'I know they are. A friend of mine plays it – well, I think she'd probably describe herself as a former friend.'

'Do it again – this time, remember, you're reaching into a ruck.'

Again, I counted down.

Three . . .

Two . . .

One!

I slipped my hand through the gap as smoothly and as quickly as I could. This time I got a hold of an egg – and this time I managed to get it out without being pecked.

'I did it!' I shouted, holding the egg up between

my thumb and forefinger. 'I didn't get pecked! I didn't get pecked!'

'Well done!' said Uncle Tim. 'That's one down! You've about another three hundred and fifty to go!'

I collected all of the eggs. It took about two hours in total, but soon I had every single one of them packed safely into seven or eight baskets.

'What's next?' I said, heading for the door. 'Milking the cows, isn't it?'

'Haven't you forgotten something?' Teresa asked.

I had forgotten something.

'Billy!' I said, smacking myself on the forehead.

I went back and picked up Billy.

'Sorry, little fella,' I said.

We headed for the cow shed. The list of jobs for the day was long and we had to keep moving to get through it.

I milked thirty cows . . .

I chased away the crows when they tried to eat the crops . . .

I got down on my hands and knees and I planted hundreds of potatoes . . .

I put straw bedding down in all the animal sheds . . .

Then I went out walking the fields for hours in search of a sheep that had gone missing.

'Come on,' Tim said as the sky was starting to darken, 'let's all go back to the house and help Auntie Kathleen with the dinner!'

'What about the chickens?' I asked. 'Don't they have to be put away?'

'Don't worry about that,' Uncle Tim said. 'You have Billy to look after. And he's hungry, by the sounds of him.'

It was true. He was bleating away in my arms: 'Ma-ha-ha-ha-ha-ha! Ma-ha-ha-ha-ha-ha!'

'I'll put the chickens away,' Clare said. 'You'll help me, Teresa, won't you?'

I carried Billy back to the house. Auntie Kathleen was in the kitchen, cooking up something that smelled wonderful, and Anne, Mary and Helena started helping her.

I sat in Uncle Tim's chair and I fed Billy another bottle of milk until he wasn't hugry anymore. Then he fell asleep on my chest. And then, quite unexpectedly, I fell asleep as well.

I woke up very suddenly with the entire family standing over me, smiling.

'Gordon?' Auntie Kathleen said. 'Your dinner's ready!'

'I'm sorry,' I said, confused for a moment. 'I must have nodded off.'

'We'll make a farmer of you yet,' Uncle Tim said.

'I'm so tired,' I said.

Then I went to sit forward and discovered that my back ached from all the work I'd done that day.

'I'm sore as well,' I added.

'But are you tired and sore in a good way?' Uncle Tim asked.

And though it seemed like a strange question to ask, when I thought about it, I realized that the answer was yes.

# 36 *Showdown!*

That was how it went for the entire week. From Monday to Friday, every day was the same. I worked with my cousins as a team. We collected the eggs. We milked the cows. We planted potatoes. We chased the crows. And I looked after Billy No Mates, making sure he was safe and warm and comfortable and well fed.

Then the strangest thing happened. Everything got easier as the week wore on. The harder I worked today, the more I could do tomorrow. Every day, I was growing fitter, stronger and sharper.

There was so much to do that I didn't have time to think about what had happened against Scotland. Or the things I'd told the *Sunday Bugle*. Or even the way I'd treated my friends.

I was busy, busy, busy.

It wasn't just Billy who was relying on me. Uncle Tim and Auntie Kathleen and all my cousins were counting on me, too. And I remembered what it was like to be part of a team again.

I was enjoying myself so much that I completely lost track of the days. I was sitting on a bale of hay one afternoon, feeding Billy from his bottle, with my cousins lounging about beside me, when Uncle Tim told us he'd just heard on the radio that Ireland had beaten England at Twickenham. It meant they now faced a showdown with Wales for the Grand Slam next weekend.

'The Grand Slam is when you win all five of your Six Nations matches,' Uncle Tim said. 'It's one of the toughest things to do in sport.'

I knew this, of course. But I hadn't even realized that Ireland were playing today. That's how far from my thoughts rugby was – it felt like it was part of my past now.

'What day is it?' I asked.

Helena and the rest of my cousins were piling the bales of hay on top of each other. She stopped what she was doing.

'It's Saturday,' she said.

I experienced this sudden sinking feeling. If it was Saturday, then this was my last day on the farm.

Uncle Tim smiled at me. 'Your dad is coming to collect you in an hour, Gordon.'

'I'm going miss this,' I said. 'I'm going to miss all of you.'

'You're welcome to come back any time,' Uncle Tim said. 'You know, you're one hell of a worker — when you put your back into it, that is.'

'I've learned so much about farming,' I said.

'I'd say you've learned one or two things about yourself as well,' suggested Uncle Tim. 'Am I right?'

I nodded.

'I'd better go and pack my bags, then,' I said.

'Not so fast,' said Clare. 'You've got one more job to do before you leave.'

'That's right,' said Mary. 'We didn't know if you were ready for it. That's why we waited until your last day.'

They were all grinning at me.

'What?' I said. 'What job?'

'You're going to have to catch Princess Layer!' Teresa said.

I felt my face break into a smile.

'Can someone look after Billy for me?' I asked.

I handed him to Anne, then I headed off in the direction of the chicken yard, with everyone following closely behind.

I reached the yard. I opened the gate, went in, then closed it behind me. The others leaned over the fence to watch. Even Auntie Kathleen came outside to see it.

The yard was full of chickens. But I recognized Princess Layer immediately. The other chickens were making a big point of ignoring me, pecking at the ground, looking for bits of corn.

But Princess Layer was standing on the opposite side of the yard, calmly taking me in. Then our eyes met and we both knew in that moment that the contest was on!

I said, 'Okay, Princess Layer – I'm putting you to bed.'

And she went:

'BOCK, BOCK, BOCK – BOOOCCCKKK!'

She was laughing at me. Or at least that's how it sounded to my ears.

I moved forward, slowly, in a sort of half-crouch, never taking my eyes off her. She didn't move a muscle until I was about six feet away from her. Then I made a dive for her and she took off to the right, half running and half flying, leaving me lying face-down in the mud.

My cousins shouted encouragement:

'Come on, Gordon! You can do it!'

I climbed to my feet again as Princess Layer strut-ted around the yard, showing off to the other chickens, who had now moved over to the side of the yard to give us space.

I dusted myself down.

'Perhaps you didn't hear me properly,' I said. 'I am here to put you to bed.'

And Princess Layer went:

'BOCK, BOCK, BOCK – BOOOCCCKKK!'

She was definitely laughing at me.

'Yeah, whatever,' I said, as I started to move towards her once more.

'Come on, Gordon!' Auntie Kathleen shouted. 'Show her who's boss!'

I shuffled forward again until I was standing about ten feet in front of her. She waited for me to make a move, to commit myself. But I didn't. I just stared into her eyes for about thirty seconds. There was pure silence. Neither of us made a noise. Neither of us made a move. We just became lost in each other's eyes. It was like we were hypnotized.

Then I moved. I pretended to lunge one way and Princess Layer made a bolt in the other direction. But I quickly corrected my position and I dived, full-length, the other way, putting my two hands around her body.

She flapped her wings and tried to peck and scratch at me. But I didn't let go of her. We rolled around on the dirt floor and she made the most awful screeching noises:

'BWWWOOOWWWKKK!!!
BWWWOOOWWWKKK!!!'

But I didn't let go of her.

She reared up in my hands and started to beat her wings wildly. Like this:

FLAP! FLAP! FLAP! FLAP! FLAP!

But I didn't let go of her. And then suddenly

something very unexpected happened. Princess Layer stopped fighting me.

'I DID IT!' I screamed, holding her aloft. 'I CAUGHT PRINCESS LAYER!'

Uncle Tim and Auntie Kathleen and my cousins all clapped.

'WELL DONE, GORDON!' they shouted. 'YOU'RE A REAL FARMER NOW!'

And Princess Layer settled happily into my arms and let me carry her off to bed. She went:

'BWOCK, BWOCK, BWOCK . . .'

But it didn't sound like mocking laughter now. It was like she was telling me that she'd enjoyed the contest and that she now respected me as a worthy opponent.

Or at least that's what I imagined. I'm going to be honest with you – I don't speak chicken.

But in that moment, finally catching Princess Layer felt better to me than beating France in Paris.

Dad collected me later that evening. I said goodbye to Uncle Tim and Auntie Kathleen, then to my cousins and to Billy No Mates. Although he wasn't

Billy No Mates anymore – because three lambs had been born that morning, so now Billy had three little playmates to keep him company.

Everyone came outside to wave me off. I said thank you and I told them that I owed them so much.

'We'll see you soon,' said Auntie Kathleen.

'Good luck with everything,' said Uncle Tim.

Then I got into the car and we drove away. Dad looked at me sideways.

'Is that a smile?' he asked. 'I haven't seen one of those in a long while! You obviously had a good time?'

'I did,' I said. 'I worked really, really hard.'

'Did you watch the Ireland v England match?'

'I didn't. I actually forgot that it was on.'

'That's very unlike you.'

'There was just so much to do. Cows to be milked. Potatoes to be planted. Eggs to be collected. There's only so many hours in a farmer's day.'

He was looking at me like he didn't recognize me.

'Well, Ireland won anyway,' he said. 'They're playing Wales next Saturday for the Grand Slam.'

'Yeah,' I said, 'I heard.'

'So are you looking forward to going back to Clongowes on Monday?'

I thought about it and I realized that I was actually excited about returning to school and normal life again.

'Yeah,' I said. 'I can't wait.'

# 37  *The Three Amigos*

It was dark when I arrived at Clongowes the following night. There was an air of excitement about the place. Friends were meeting up again and exchanging stories about what they'd gotten up to on their break. Everyone was really buzzing.

As I walked through the lobby, I braced myself for the worst. I was expecting to hear more of the same jokes and comments as before. People laughing about my golden boots. My green hair. The things I'd said in the *Sunday Bugle*.

But, as I made my way through the crowd of boys, something very surprising happened:

Nothing!

That's right! Nothing at all!

No one said anything to me – good, bad or indifferent. It was like no one even remembered that I'd ever played for Ireland. Like the whole thing was something that happened AGES and AGES ago and life had moved on and it didn't matter anymore.

I made my way to the dormitories. As I reached the door of my room, I heard voices coming from inside.

One voice was saying: 'I can't believe you're back studying already! Would you not take the night off?'

And the other voice was saying: 'Did you know there are only forty-eight days of school left before the summer exams?'

I pushed the door and I walked in. I couldn't believe it. Conor was lying on the bottom bunk. Peter was sitting at his study desk. They'd clearly moved back in.

'I'm sorry,' I said, 'I'll find another room,' and I went to leave.

'Where do you think you're going?' Conor asked.

'I was going to find somewhere else to sleep,' I said. 'That's if we're never going to be friends again.'

Conor stood up from his bed.

'We *are* going to be friends again,' he said. 'We can be friends now if you like.'

I could have cried at that moment. To be honest, I did – just a little bit.

Peter stood up from his desk. That was a HUGE

moment in itself — like he said, the summer exams were only a matter of weeks away. He stuck out his hand for me to shake it. I swatted it out of the way and gave him a hug instead. Then Conor joined in.

'I'm so sorry for the way I acted,' I said.

'Forget it,' Conor said.

'I'm sorry. I can't say it enough times.'

'Once is plenty,' Peter said.

'Let's put the whole thing behind us,' Conor suggested.

'I'd like that,' I said. 'I really would.'

'That's good. Because I've got an idea for a prank.'

I laughed. I'd really missed this.

'What is it?' I asked, drying my eyes with the back of my hand.

'Okay, listen,' he said.

I listened.

'What am I listening to?' I said.

'Shush, shush,' he said.

And that's when we heard a loud, 'MOO-OOOOOOOO!' coming from outside. It was Bessie the Cow, who lived in a field next to the school.

'Okay, what are you planning?' Peter asked nervously.

'*We*,' Conor stressed, 'are going to wait until

everyone has gone to bed – then we're going to bring Bessie the Cow . . . INTO THE SCHOOL!'

I laughed. It was a brilliant idea.

'No!' Peter insisted. 'I want nothing to do with this!'

'Come on!' Conor said. 'You have to have some fun while you're here, Peter! You know what they say about all work and no play!'

Conor and I spent the next hour working on Peter until he finally agreed to help us. Then, shortly after the bell sounded for Lights Out, Conor quietly opened the door and looked up and down the corridor.

'It's dark,' he whispered. 'Let's go.'

As silently as we could, we tiptoed out of the dorm . . .

Along the corridor . . .

Through the emergency fire door . . .

And outside . . .

Keeping as close to the walls and as out of sight as possible, we made our way around the back of the school . . .

Then we crossed the car park, using the six or seven cars parked there as cover . . .

Until we reached the field, where Bessie was munching on the grass without a care in the world. She was a friendly old thing. I patted her on the head while Peter opened the farm gate and Conor encouraged her forward by showing her a handful of grass.

'Come on, Bessie!' he said. 'How would you like to spend the night in the warmth for once?'

She followed us like an obedient dog, across the car park . . .

Around the outside of the school . . .

Through the emergency door . . .

Down the corridor of the dormitory block . . .

And all the time, I was thinking, Please don't moo, Bessie! Please! Do not! Moo!

We led her out of the dormitory block . . .

Then through the lobby . . .

Then left, down one hallway . . .

Then right, down another hallway . . .

And into the staffroom . . . where we left her, looking delighted with herself, happy to be in out of the cold and chewing away on the teachers' plants.

I looked at Conor and Peter and we all laughed. I was so happy that we were friends again and it was great to be back doing normal things.

Well, that's if you could call this normal.

'Try to be as quiet as you can,' Conor told Bessie. 'Trust me – when the teachers walk in and see you here, it's going to be HILARIOUS!'

Then the three of us crept back to our room.

## 38 Rumbled!

We were awoken by the sound of a woman screaming. It went like this:

'AAAAAARRRRRRGGGGGGGHHHHH!!!'

Lying in my coffin, I could hear the sound of doors being thrown open. Up and down the corridor, I could hear boys, barely awake, asking, 'What's going on?' and 'Who's screaming?'

It turned out to be Mrs Hudd, the Geography teacher, because, a second or two later, she was running up and down the corridor, shouting:

'THERE'S A COW IN THE STAFFROOM! THERE'S A COW IN THE STAFFROOM!'

I looked over the side of my coffin down at Conor and we were suddenly helpless with laughter. Even Peter laughed – and that was saying something.

Then I started to hear the titters, then the giggles, then the outright hoots from the other boys up and down the corridor. It was immediately clear that this was even funnier than drawing moustaches on everyone in the class with semi-permanent markers. Because this time, the entire school seemed to find it HILARIOUS.

Plus, the great advantage of this prank was that there was absolutely nothing to link it to us!

I heard Mr Cuffe's voice in the hallway outside. He was shouting:

'I WANT EVERY STUDENT IN THIS DORMITORY TO BE DRESSED AND

STANDING IN THE ASSEMBLY HALL IN EXACTLY FIVE MINUTES!'

We quickly put on our clothes.

'We'd better MOOOOOVE it!' said Conor.

He really was hilarious.

Four minutes and fifty-nine seconds later, we were standing in the assembly hall, waiting to find out what was going to happen.

Mr Cuffe was standing at the top of the room, along with Father Billings and Bessie the Cow, who actually looked quite happy with her new surroundings.

We lined up the same way we did after the moustache incident. Again, Mr Cuffe walked up and down the line, staring into our faces, and said:

'Last night, once again, a boy – or boys – brought disgrace on this institute of learning by behaving like a ruffian. Or ruffians.'

'Oh my God,' Conor said out of the side of his mouth, 'he's really *milking* this, isn't he?'

I burst out laughing. I couldn't help it.

'SILENCE!' Mr Cuffe said.

Father Billings shook his head – again, in a disappointed way.

*PPPPPPHHHHHHFFFFFFAAAAAAR-RRRRRTTTTTT!!!!!!!*

It was very hard to keep a straight face.

'I want to give the person or persons responsible the opportunity to come clean,' said Mr Cuffe. 'If you were involved in bringing livestock into the school staffroom, then step forward now!'

Beside me, Conor whispered, 'Don't step forward! Pretend it was someone *udder* than us!'

I had to put my hand over my mouth.

'Fine,' said Mr Cuffe, 'it looks like we're not going to get a confession. However, it wouldn't take the world's greatest genius to figure out who was responsible.'

No way, I thought. This time we definitely didn't leave any loose ends – did we?

Mr Cuffe said, 'Would every boy in the assembly hall who *hasn't* got mud on his shoes please sit down?'

I looked down. My shoes were caked in mud. So were Conor's. And so were Peter's. Everyone else sat down. We remained standing.

Father Billings smiled at us sadly.

*PPPPPPHHHHHHHFFFFFFAAAAAAR-RRRRRTTTTTT!!!!!!!*

'You three, come with me,' Mr Cuffe said. 'I'm sure I can find an appropriate punishment for each of you!'

Mr Cuffe was very imaginative when it came to dreaming up new and interesting punishments for the students who had crossed the line.

First, he fixed his eyes on Peter.

'You, boy,' he said. 'I have a very important job for you.'

'What is it, Sir?' Peter asked.

'I want you to count every single floor tile in the entire school.'

Peter didn't seem upset by that at all – probably because he loved maths.

'That's fine,' he said.

'I have given this punishment to three students previously,' Mr Cuffe told him, 'and after seven hours of counting, they each came up with exactly the same number. So you won't be able to cheat by making up a figure.'

'I'll get to work right away, Sir.'

Mr Cuffe turned to Conor then. 'You, boy, can go to the school stationery shop,' he said, 'and do a complete inventory of all the stock.'

Conor's face lit up.

'That's alright,' he said. 'That's not bad at all.'

'You will count every single paper clip, staple and elastic band individually and you will provide an accurate figure.'

That was different.

'But, Sir,' Conor complained, 'that's going to take me hours! Maybe even days!'

'Then you'd better get started,' Mr Cuffe said.

He looked at me then.

'Ah,' he said, 'the boy who played rugby for Ireland! I've got the perfect punishment for you! Because, in a way, it's rugby-related!'

He produced a scissors.

'I want you to cut the grass on the main rugby pitch,' he said.

'WHAT?' I was sure I'd misheard him.

'It's getting a bit long,' he said. 'Hasn't been cut since before the holidays. I want you to see to it — every single blade!'

There was no point in arguing with him. I took the scissors from him and I went outside.

I couldn't believe it. Conor was great at thinking up ideas for pranks, but we REALLY had to become better at covering our tracks.

Half an hour later, I was down on my hands and knees, snipping away at the grass, making VERY slow progress. And that was when I heard voices.

The voices of girls.

Oh, no! I thought. Please don't let it be her! PLEASE don't let it be HER!

But it was her.

I looked up to see Aoife and the rest of the St Bridget's team walking towards me. They were clearly planning to train this morning.

Aoife laughed when she saw me down on my hands and knees with the scissors.

'Oh my God!' she said. 'What are you DOING?'

I tried to put a brave face on it. I pretended it was something I'd chosen to do of my own free will.

'We were playing here last night,' I said, 'and I noticed there was an area of grass that was a bit on the long side.'

'He's talking rubbish!' one of the girls said. 'It was obviously another one of your cousin's pranks, Aoife!'

I decided to come clean then.

'We brought Bessie the Cow into the staffroom,' I said. 'We got caught because we forgot to wipe the mud off our shoes.'

'How the mighty have fallen!' another one of the girls said.

Aoife laughed.

'I suppose we should be honoured that he's even talking to us,' she said. 'Are you sure you don't want us to direct our questions through your agent, Gordon?'

Ouch! I thought. But I deserved it.

'Look,' I said, still down on my knees, 'I'm really sorry about the way I treated you – the way I treated all of you.'

Aoife looked at her teammates.

'What do you think, girls?' she asked. 'Should we forgive him?'

'As long as he does a good job on the grass,' one of them answered.

Aoife laughed.

'Okay,' she said. 'We're friends again.'

I stood up and we made it official with hand-shakes all round.

'My offer still stands,' I told them. 'If you need any coaching . . .'

'Thanks for the offer,' Aoife said, 'but I think we're doing fine by ourselves. You can come and watch us play if you want. We have our very first match against St Theresa's this Saturday.'

'I'll be there,' I told her. 'And that's a promise.'

# 39 *Retired*

It was Free Time on Wednesday night. I was in the dorm, sitting at my study desk, when Conor and Peter walked in.

'What are you doing?' Conor asked.

'Oh, I'm just catching up on some Geography,' I told him.

'No, what I mean is why aren't you changed for rugby? It's Wednesday!'

I didn't know how to break the news to him.

'Conor, I've made a decision,' I said. 'I've decided I don't want to play rugby anymore.'

'WHAT?' he said.

'I've decided to retire,' I told him.

'You can't retire. Come on, you're too good.'

'I'm not, Conor. Let's be honest, I got lucky. And

then I made a complete fool of myself in front of the whole country.'

'Peter, can you talk to this fella, please?'

'Gordon,' Peter said, 'I know you had a bad experience. But you love rugby.'

'To tell you the truth,' I said, 'I'm not really sure I do anymore.'

I was telling the truth. Perhaps my nerve had gone. But I had lost my appetite for the game. I didn't care whether I ever held a ball in my hands again.

Peter did something that I wasn't expecting then. He took my Geography book away from me.

'What are you doing?' I asked.

'There are more important things in life,' he said, 'than sitting in your room with your nose in a book all night.'

'This coming from you? Really?'

'Just come outside with us,' he said. 'You don't have to play – just watch.'

'You could give us one or two tips,' Conor suggested. 'Things you learned during your time with the Ireland squad.'

I laughed.

'The only thing I learned,' I said, 'was how to mess up a once-in-a-lifetime opportunity.'

'You're not getting this book back,' Peter said, 'so you might as well come with us. The air will do you good.'

I had no choice but to follow them outside. I had no intention of playing, though. I was still in my school uniform.

I stood there, happy to just watch, while the other boys warmed up.

Mr Murray arrived then.

'Hi, Gordon,' he said. 'You're not joining us, no?'

'No,' I told him. 'I've given up.'

'Given up rugby?' he said. 'You're very young to make such a big life decision. You might feel differently one day.'

'I don't think I will.'

'Please yourself.'

He emptied the bibs out onto the ground and the boys all made a dive for them. Then the match started. I watched, only half interested.

They'd been playing for about ten minutes when Peter got the ball in his hands. Then he did the second thing that day that surprised me. He hoofed the ball high into the air and out of touch. I couldn't understand why he did it. But then I realized that it was coming towards me. It was falling out of the sky fast.

Instinctively, without even thinking about it, I turned my body sideways, without ever taking my eyes off the ball. Then I put my hands in the air and waited for it as it came . . .

Spinning . . .

Spinning . . .

Spinning . . .

And then . . .

BOOOMP!

I caught it! I caught it cleanly!

All of the boys cheered.

Peter had kicked the ball in my direction purposely, knowing that I'd have to catch it, knowing that I couldn't help myself.

And now I felt myself smile. And, in that moment, my confidence returned. And I suddenly had the urge to play rugby again.

'What are you going to do with that ball?' Conor shouted.

I threw him a long pass. It was the same long pass I threw to Rob Kearney against Scotland – the one that was intercepted and cost us a try. But this time it sailed over everyone's heads and landed safely in Conor's hands. He didn't even have to move.

'Have you changed your mind?' Mr Murray asked.

And I just nodded.

'I'll just go back to the dorm,' I said, 'and change into my rugby gear.'

My feet couldn't carry me fast enough.

# 40 *Expect the Unexpected*

It was Thursday morning. I was in the cafeteria, queuing for breakfast with Conor and Peter. The queue was moving at a snail's pace. As usual, we were worried that we wouldn't have time to eat a thing before the bell sounded for the first class of the day.

All of a sudden, two boys brushed past us on the way to the front of the queue.

'Hey!' Peter yelled. 'You can't skip the line!'

'Yeah,' added Conor, 'we've been standing here for the last twenty minutes!'

The two boys turned around. It was Flash Barry – and with him was his newest client.

'This is Steven Varsey!' Barry said. 'He's going to be playing at Junior Wimbledon this summer – he doesn't have time to be standing around in queues!'

Maybe it was my imagination, but Steven Varsey seemed to have put on quite a bit of weight since I last saw him.

Steven rolled his eyes, shook his head impatiently and said, 'Can we get a move on here? I don't have time to be standing around talking to complete nobodies.'

A second of two later, I heard him ask Janice for thirty-seven sausages.

By the time *we* reached the top of the queue, all that was left was a few measly beans. We only had time to eat two forkfuls each before the bell sounded.

'Come on,' Peter said, 'we can't be late! It's Double Maths!'

A few minutes later, we were about to walk into the classroom when I heard my name called. I turned around. It was Mr Murray.

'Gordon!' he said. 'I just heard the news on the radio in the staffroom! It's fantastic!'

I had no idea what he was talking about.

'What do you mean?' I asked.

'Are you saying you haven't heard?' he said.

'Heard what?'

'Gordon, you're back in the Ireland squad!'

'WHAT?'

'It said on the news that Kevin Maggs was injured.

Warren Gatland has no other options in the centre. He's recalled you, Gordon!'

I felt someone slap me very hard across the back. It was Conor. He let a loud . . . 'WAH-OOOOOO!!!!!!' . . . out of him.

I didn't know *how* to react. I was in shock.

Peter said, 'It's great news, Gordon. I really am delighted for you.'

Mr Murray was excited, too.

'I told you,' he said, 'that you'd get another chance? The difference this time is that you'll be ready for it!'

Conor said, 'I don't believe it! I DON'T BELIEVE IT! You're going to be playing against Wales on Saturday – for the Grand Slam, Darce!'

I was starting to get excited. But then I remembered something that brought me back to Earth again.

'I can't play,' I said.

'WHAT?' said Conor.

'Why not?' Mr Murray asked.

'St Bridget's are playing St Theresa's on Saturday afternoon,' I said.

'Okay – and which one have you been picked to play for?' asked Conor.

'Neither,' I said. 'But I promised Aoife and the rest of the Bridget's team that I'd be there to watch.'

'Have you lost your mind?' Conor said. 'You've got an opportunity here to win the Six Nations – with IRELAND!'

'This is the second chance we talked about,' Mr Murray said. 'Think long and hard about it before you turn it down.'

'It would mean breaking a promise and letting down a friend,' I said. 'I don't want to do that again, so I'm going to say no.'

# 41 'Warren Gatland Just Rang the House!'

I was in Double Geography when there was an announcement over the intercom that I was to go to Mr Cuffe's office. I wondered did it have something to do with the poor job I'd made of the task he'd given me?

Do you know how long it takes to cut the grass on an entire rugby field with a scissors? You should try it some time!

In seven hours, I didn't get more than a small square completed – and that was what I thought Mr Cuffe wanted to talk about when I was summoned to his office.

But it had nothing to do with that at all. He said there was a telephone call for me and he pointed at the receiver lying on his desk.

Mr Cuffe left me alone and I picked it up slowly.

'Hello?' I said.

'Gordon!' a voice said. 'You're back in the Ireland squad!'

It was Dad, sounding *very* excited.

'Hi, Dad,' I said. 'Yeah, apparently it was on the news.'

'Not only was it on the news,' he said, 'Warren Gatland just rang the house. He was talking to your mother. He said they're going to be training tomorrow morning at the Aviva Stadium – and he wants *you* to be there!'

'Right.'

'Right? You don't sound too excited, Gordon. Are you in shock or something?'

'No, it's just that Saturday doesn't really suit me?'

'Doesn't suit you? It's the Six Nations decider!'

'I know.'

'The Grand Slam is at stake!'

'I know that, too.'

'So what do you mean it doesn't suit you?'

'My friend is playing for St Bridget's against St Theresa's on Saturday.'

'St Bridget's?'

'Yeah.'

'Against St Theresa's?'

'Yeah, there's a fixtures clash.'

'God, I wonder does Warren Gatland know? He might be able to move the Grand Slam decider to another day!'

'Don't be sarcastic, Dad.'

'Sorry, Gordon. It's just, this is your opportunity to put what happened against Scotland behind you once and for all.'

'But it would mean letting down a friend – and I've let down too many people already.'

Dad was silent for a moment, then he said, 'You're right, Gordon. I'll ring Warren Gatland tonight and tell him that you're not available.'

I could tell from his voice that he was disappointed.

'Thanks, Dad,' I said.

'I'll talk to you soon,' he said, then he hung up.

I left the office and started walking back to class. And that was when I met Mr Murray. He was pushing the paint-rolling machine that was used to mark the rugby pitch.

'Ah, Gordon,' he said. 'I was wondering if you could do me a small favour?'

'Yeah,' I said, 'what is it?'

'Well, as you mentioned earlier,' he said, 'St

Bridget's are playing St Theresa's this weekend and I was thinking maybe it would be a nice gesture if we marked the pitch for them.'

'You want ME to mark the pitch?'

'That's okay, isn't it? Unless you consider it beneath you?'

'No, not at all. It's just I should be in Double Geography.'

'I'll talk to your teacher and say I gave you a little job to do.'

'Okay,' I said, 'fine.'

I made my way outside and I pushed the paint-roller in the direction of the main pitch. I noticed that Aoife was there, practising her kicking as usual. She stopped when she saw me.

'Hi,' she said. 'It said on the radio that you're back in the Ireland squad?'

'Yeah,' I said, 'Warren Gatland was talking to my mum.'

'You know it's on the same day as our match? Ours kicks off half an hour after the Grand Slam game ends.'

'I know that,' I said. 'That's why I've decided not to play.'

'Good,' she said.

'What?'

I was surprised to hear her say it.

'You promised to come and see us play,' she said, 'so that's what you should do.'

'I know,' I said. 'Look, I better get on with marking the pitch.'

I'd walked about ten steps with the paint-roller when I suddenly heard her say:

'Are you absolutely INSANE?'

I turned back.

'What do you mean?' I asked.

'What do I mean? You've been given the chance to play for Ireland again and you're going to turn it down? Why?'

'Because you're my friend. And your match is a big deal as well.'

She looked at me for a moment, then she smiled. 'Well, that's pretty incredible of you, but what kind of a friend would I be if I asked you to give up an opportunity like that?'

'I said I'd be there, and I will be,' I said. 'I don't want to make the same mistakes again.'

'You won't,' Aoife said gently. 'Gordon, I am telling you to go and play for Ireland. And make us all proud of you, okay?'

I looked over and I saw Mr Murray smiling in our direction. Did he ask me to mark the pitch because he knew that me and Aoife would end up having this conversation? It seemed so. I smiled back at him.

'I won't let you down,' I said. 'I won't let any of you down.'

## 42  *Mad Men*

I was quiet in the car as we drove to the Aviva Stadium for training the following morning. Dad asked me if I was okay and I lied.

'Yeah,' I said, 'I'm fine.'

He saw right through it, of course.

'You're bound to be nervous,' he said. 'It's entirely natural.'

But I was *more* than just nervous. I was TER-RIFIED. I hadn't seen any of the Ireland players since I'd made such an eejit of myself against Scotland. In my mind, I kept returning to that moment when I was lying on the ground and no one offered me a hand to help me up.

'What if THEY haven't forgiven me?' I asked.

'That's their choice,' Dad said. 'And if that *is* the

case, it's something you're just going to have to deal with.'

'I don't know if I can face them,' I said.

Dad turned the car into the stadium car park. When he pulled up, I stayed sitting in the front passenger seat.

'I've changed my mind,' I said. 'Drive me back to Clongowes, will you?'

Dad just smiled.

'I will,' he said, 'if that's what you really want. But let me just say this to you first – you've already done the hardest bit, Gordon.'

'Have I?' I asked.

'When you went back to school after the Scotland match. Do you remember that? Your mother and I dropped you off outside. You took a deep breath, then you went in to face all your schoolmates. That took real bravery, Gordon. And your mother said to me, "That boy has got so much more courage than he knows."'

'Did she really say that?'

'She did.'

I stared through the windscreen at the door of the dressing room.

'Okay,' I said. 'Here goes!'

I got out of the car and took my kit bag from the boot. Then I headed for that door. My heart was beating so hard. It was going:

BA-DOOM!  BA-DOOM!  BA-DOOM! BA-DOOM!

And my mouth was dry. I was really nervous. But still I pushed open the door and went inside.

The dressing room was full. No one seemed to notice me when I came in. They were all too busy getting changed and slagging each other. That was a huge relief because it allowed me to slip quietly into the corner and pretend to be invisible.

I sat down on a bench and unzipped my kit bag – and I got the fright of my life. Because inside the bag, staring up at me, were the boots . . .

Yes, THOSE boots . . .

The golden ones with 'TOTAL' and 'LEGEND' written across them.

I didn't know what to do. I had nothing else to wear. My instinct was to run for the door.

'Here!' a voice said.

I looked up. It was ROG. He was handing me a pair of boots.

'These are my spares,' he said. 'You can wear them today. And tomorrow – provided you're picked, that is!'

That was when the other players started to notice me.

'Have you done something to your hair?' BOD asked, a big smirk on his face.

'Er, no,' I said, 'this is my natural colour.'

'I think I actually preferred it green,' said Strings. Everyone laughed.

I decided I needed to say something – to own my actions.

'Look, I want to apologize to all of you,' I said, 'for the way I behaved. Walking out of training that day in Greystones – it was very disrespectful to the rest of you. Same with eating all those sausages every morning and that bucket of nachos with cheese.'

'What about the things you said about us in the *Sunday Bugle*?' Rob Kearney asked.

'Yeah, I was coming to that,' I told him. 'Just because I played well once, I let myself think I was a star. I forgot that being good at anything requires hard work. I let myself down – and I let all of you down. And I want you to know that I've learned my lesson and I'm truly sorry.'

They all stared at me in silence, and I could feel my face going red. Then Paulie stood up and walked towards me, his hand held out for me to shake.

'Apology accepted,' he said. 'On behalf of us all, you're welcome back to the fold, Darce.'

And just like that, the past was forgotten.

'Okay,' Paulie said, 'we're playing for the Grand Slam tomorrow! Let's go out there and train like MAD MEN!'

Train like mad men we certainly did! First, we warmed up. Then we did all of the usual drills. Except this time we did them for longer – and with more intensity. Warren kept telling us, 'Remember, however hard you think you're working, Wales are doing what you're doing – plus twenty percent more!'

And that made us dig even deeper within ourselves.

We practised our set moves again. I was in the same group as the last time I trained with the team in Greystones. It was BOD, ROG, Rob Kearney and me. We practised the miss-pass. It was the move that had been my final undoing against Scotland – the pass that Kenny Logan had intercepted just before I was substituted. I was determined now to become the best miss-passer in the entire world. So we did it over and over and over again until we got it right ten times in a row. But this time, I was the one saying that we should keep going.

'Let's see can we do it right TWENTY times in a row!' I suggested.

BOD winked at me. 'You're sure you're not too tired?' he asked.

'I'm fine to keep going,' I said, 'as long as you guys are.'

So we kept going. We did it again. Then again.

Then again. Until it felt like it was a dance routine. Until we knew how it should feel every time we did it – the timing, the rhythm, the pace of the move.

We finished. I looked across at the sideline. I could see Dad smiling at me. He was pleased for me.

We took a quick breather. While we did, ROG poked me in the belly with his finger.

'You've lost weight, boy,' he commented.

'Thanks,' I said – because I presumed he meant it as a compliment.

'What's your secret?' he wanted to know. 'You must have been in the gym twelve hours a day, were you?'

'No,' I said. 'I was working on my Uncle Tim and Auntie Kathleen's farm.'

He laughed. 'Working on a farm?'

'Yeah,' I said. 'I was planting potatoes and chasing crows and catching chickens and milking cows.'

'I didn't even know you boys had farms in Leinster.'

'Plus, I've been eating more sensibly,' I told him. 'I've kind of gone off sausages. And cheese nachos.'

We got back to work then. We practised the wrap switch. We did the same thing. We did it once, then we kept on doing it, until it became second nature to us. I noticed that Warren was watching me carefully, but he didn't say anything.

Then we took another short break. I was parched. Rob went to the cooler box and got us each an energy drink.

'Is that okay for you?' he asked me. 'You don't want to grab a Cokanta-Up from the limo, do you?'

All I could do was laugh.

'No,' ROG reminded him, 'the Cokanta-Ups make him burpy, don't forget!'

I would NEVER live that episode down! But it's actually a relief sometimes to have a good laugh at yourself.

BOD and ROG started having an argument then about who was the fastest sprinter on the Ireland team.

'That's easy,' ROG said. 'It's me.'

BOD laughed. 'Yeah, you're dreaming,' he told him. 'How many times have I left you eating my dust when I was playing for Leinster and you were playing for Munster?'

'Only when you've had a headstart,' ROG argued.

'That's rubbish,' BOD told him. 'You've never beaten me in a race for the ball. Ever.'

Rob got involved then. 'There's very little between you two,' he said. 'But, let's be honest, I'm faster than both of you.'

Some of the others players started to get interested

then. The Munster guys all reckoned ROG was the fastest, but the Leinster guys thought it was with either BOD or Rob.

Paulie said that Strings was also fast.

Warren said there was one way to settle the argument once and for all. He told all of the backs to line up at one end of the pitch. We were going to race each other over one hundred yards to see who was the fastest player in the squad. Whoever crossed the tryline at the other end of the field first was the winner.

We stood behind the line. We all got down on one knee, with the palms of our hands flat on the ground, like the sprinters you see in the Olympics.

'On your marks . . .' Warren shouted. 'Set . . .'

We lifted our knees off the ground.

'Go!' Warren shouted.

BOD, ROG and Rob took off like three express trains. They flew out of the blocks. I was immediately staring at the backs of their heads while pumping my arms and legs really, REALLY hard.

On the sidelines, the forwards watched. I heard Sean O'Brien shout, 'Rob has it!' but Paul O'Connell said, 'No way – ROG has this!' and Cian Healy said, 'No way! Watch BOD turn on the after-burners any second now!'

I kept going. And somewhere around the midway point, I noticed that I was gaining on them.

'Rob has slowed up!' Devin Toner shouted. 'He's gone, look!'

A second later, I passed Rob Kearney. ROG was in the lead, followed by BOD, then I was immediately behind them in third.

With about twenty-five metres to go, I passed out BOD. For the first time, the guys on the sideline seemed to notice me.

'Look at Darce!' Paulie shouted. 'He's flying, look!'

I heard Dad's voice then. He shouted, 'Go on, Gordon! Go on! You can do it!'

There were twenty metres to go and I was closing the gap on ROG. He had a quick glance over his shoulder at me and I saw the look of surprise on his face to see me gaining on him.

He tried to find another gear, but he was spent from all the effort. We were just a few feet from the line when I passed him out and I dipped my head to make sure I crossed the line first. There was no more than a couple of inches between us.

The other players cheered.

'Well done, Darce!' they shouted.

I collapsed on the grass in the in-goal area. ROG

collapsed, too, a few feet away from me. We were both gasping for breath.

'Do you know something?' ROG said when he'd finally got his breath back. 'I think I preferred you when you were on the sausages and the cheese nachos!'

Again, I had to laugh.

When training was over, the only thing that Warren said to me was: 'Well done, Gordon. See you tomorrow.'

And that was it.

Dad walked over to me. 'Well?' he said.

'Well, what?' I asked.

'I saw Warren talking to you just now. Are you in the team for the Wales match?'

'I don't know.'

'What do you mean, you don't know?'

'He didn't tell me. He just said well done and he'd see me tomorrow.'

'He didn't say anything more than that?'

'No.'

'I suppose we'll just have to keep our fingers crossed until just before kick-off tomorrow, then.'

I wanted to be in the starting XV for the Grand Slam decider. I really did. But whether I was or not, I was very happy with the morning's work I'd done.

Even if I didn't get on the pitch against Wales, I felt like I'd achieved something.

But then . . . who am I kidding?

I really, REALLY wanted to play.

# 43  *The Game of My Life*

Warren broke the news to me on the morning of the match.

'You're in the team,' he told me.

I smiled. Or maybe it was more of a grin. I was so happy to hear those words.

'Let me finish,' he said. 'You're in the team . . . because we're desperate. You're in the team because Kevin is injured and there's no one else. I'm not going to lie to you, Gordon, I still have major reservations about you. You played one good game for Ireland and it all went to your head.'

'I know,' I said.

'I haven't forgotten that day at Greystones when you walked out of training. What did you say you were?'

'Burpy.'

'Burpy – that's right. And you saw the consequences of that against Scotland. You hadn't put the work in and you were exhausted, which meant you were useless to the team.'

'I learned my lesson.'

'I hope so. Because it isn't just me giving you a second chance today – it's all of your teammates as well.'

'I won't blow it,' I said. 'I promise.'

'Alright,' he said, still sounding uncertain, 'just go out there and do your best.'

The time flew by until kick-off. I tried to keep my focus, which meant having to forget about everything that was going on around the match.

Eighty minutes of rugby. That was all I kept thinking during the national anthems. I blanked out the music from the Garda band and the cheering of the crowd and all the talk of winning the Six Nations Championship and the Grand Slam and I just focused on the match. Because that's all this was, I told myself.

One match.

Eighty minutes of rugby.

The referee blew the whistle and the ball was suddenly in the air.

It was on!

We spent the first ten minutes just feeling each other out. Wales kicked the ball deep into our half, then we caught it and kicked it right back into theirs. That sometimes happens in a match when two teams are trying to get the measure of each other. You're both trying to force each other into making a mistake so you can use the error to your advantage.

We won a penalty for an infringement in the scrum and ROG kicked us into a 3–0 lead. But then Neil Jenkins, the Welsh outhalf, kicked a penalty and we were level again.

It was one of those first halves that was too tense for anyone in the crowd to really enjoy it. And it was hard work for us.

I got tackled . . .

Then I made a tackle . . .

Then I got tackled again . . .

It went on like this for the entire first half. It was like a war out there. I was exhausted and sore all over, but I didn't let it show. It felt like all of the hard work that I'd put into collecting eggs and milking cows and planting potatoes and chasing crows and putting the chickens to bed had given me the ability to deal with the aches and the pains and the tiredness.

And then something really amazing happened. I found myself lying on the ground after a tackle by the Welsh number eight, Scott Quinnell . . .

A VERY hard tackle . . .

I was feeling dazed and winded. And then all these Irish hands appeared to help me up. At that moment, I knew that I was truly back in the team.

Just before half-time, I had the ball in my hands and I noticed that ROG was standing a little back from the play, shouting at me, 'THE DROP, DARCE! THE DROP!', which meant he thought he had the chance to score with a drop goal. So I made the pass. ROG caught it and launched it with his foot in the direction of the goal. The ball seemed to wobble through the air. I held my breath as I watched it hit the inside of the post and then, to everyone's great relief, go over the bar for another three points.

We were winning 6–3 at half-time. In the dressing room, Warren told us to keep doing what we were doing and that an opening would come as the Welsh got tired.

Then he looked at me and said, 'That forty

minutes you've just put in – THAT was the Gordon D'Arcy I saw play for Clongowes.'

I felt like my heart was on fire with pride! I was going to go out there and play the very best rugby I could – for Warren, for Ireland, and for me.

We went back out onto the field. Forty minutes more, I told myself. Forty minutes more. And we went at it again.

Warren was right. As the two teams tired, the game opened up a bit. It meant that when you got the ball in your hands, you had a little bit more time to think about what you were going to do with it.

And that's what happened fifteen minutes into the second half when I collected a pass from Strings and I could see that the Welsh defence was stretched. As a matter of fact, I could see a gap in front of me that I reckoned I could squeeze through . . .

Possibly . . .

It was fifty–fifty . . .

Or maybe forty–sixty . . .

Okay, it was an outside chance, but if I managed to slip between those two players, I would score a try and be the hero of the hour – just like I was in Paris. Man of the Match!

But then, out of the corner of my eye, I spotted Rob Kearney to my right, charging forward and calling for the ball. He was in a far better position to score than I was.

Time slowed down . . .

I thought about my options . . .

Do the right thing for me . . .

Or the right thing for the team?

I flung the ball to Rob, who caught it, then a few seconds later he dived over the line to score a try.

The noise in the stadium was deafening. Rob ran straight to me to thank me for the pass. We celebrated the try, but we didn't lose the run of ourselves because we knew we were still in a match.

ROG added the conversion to put us 13–3 ahead.

But then Wales came back at us like we knew they would. They answered us back with two penalties and as the game entered the final stages they just needed a try to win the Six Nations Championship and the Grand Slam.

With only a few seconds left to play, Neil Jenkins got his hands on the ball and ran at our defensive line. He slipped one tackle . . .

Then another . . .

In the blink of an eye he'd managed to get in behind us and he was pelting for the line. I was chasing after him, but he was fast. I could hear the Ireland supporters groan because there were only thirty metres between him and a certain try under the posts. And five points plus two for the conversion would give Wales victory – and break our hearts.

And that's when I realized that I was the nearest player to Jenkins. I was the only Ireland player close enough to catch him. But it was going to take a huge effort because he was so quick. As a matter of fact, he reminded of . . .

And that's when I had a flashback . . .

. . . to chasing Princess Layer around the farmyard in Wexford.

When I looked down at Neil's legs, I could see he had . . .

Chicken legs!

That's right! Above the waist, he was Neil Jenkins, the Welsh rugby player. But below the waist, he was a farmyard chicken.

I gritted my teeth and I ran as fast as I could and I knew that I was closing the distance between us. The noise of the crowd rose to fever-pitch as they noticed that I was gaining on the man with the ball. But he was getting closer to the tryline . . .

Ten metres . . .

Five metres . . .

Then . . .

I threw myself at him like I threw myself at

Princess Layer. I hit him hard around the waist and he fell just short of the line.

The ball squirmed out of his hands.

And for a moment that seemed to go on forever, we both lay there on the ground, staring at that ball, lying just a few feet away, wondering who would arrive on the scene first. Would it be another Welsh player to ground the ball under the posts? Or would it be . . .

In a blur of green, ROG raced by and he kicked the ball out of play.

We had won!

We had beaten Wales!

We had won the Six Nations Championship and the Grand Slam!

'Could you not have tackled him a few metres earlier?' ROG asked, a big smirk on his face as he helped me up. 'Would have saved us all an awful lot of stress, like!'

Paulie clapped me on the back. 'That was one hell of a shift you put in today,' he said.

And BOD hugged me and said, 'We wouldn't have won it without you, Darce.'

Warren stuck out his hand to me. 'Congratulations, Darce. You just played the game of your life.'

And in that moment, I felt that I'd finally made

up for all the stupid mistakes I'd made in letting my success go to my head.

I looked around me. The crowd was going mad. Very few of them had ever seen Ireland win a Grand Slam before. It was such a rare thing that many of them must have known they might never see it happen again. People were openly weeping. I have to admit, I had a bit of a cry myself.

I mean, you would, too, wouldn't you?

A stage appeared in the middle of the pitch. I didn't even see anyone set it up. It was just suddenly there. We were told that that was where we would be receiving the Six Nations trophy from President Michael D. Higgins.

It felt like a dream.

ROG put his arm around my shoulder and whispered in my ear: 'I'm trying to imagine just how big your head is going to be after this, Darce!'

'No way,' I said. 'I won't be getting carried away like that again!'

Warren told us they were ready to present the trophy, so we walked over to the stage and lined up. I stood near to the back. One by one, we stepped onto the stage and we were each handed a medal on a piece of green ribbon. I hung mine around my neck, then I stared at that medal. And, though it might seem like a strange thing to say, I felt the same way about that medal as I did about the roast potatoes on Uncle Tim and Auntie Kathleen's farm. I knew that I'd earned it. I knew I hadn't cheated anyone.

BOD was about to receive the trophy. I was standing at the back of the stage, behind the giant figures of Cian Healy and Sean O'Brien. Paulie looked around him.

'Where's Darce?' he asked. 'Darce, get up here to the front where people can see you.'

Lots of pairs of hands pushed me forward. I stood next to BOD as the President walked over to him with the Six Nations trophy. It was so big and so shiny! In the crowd, I could see hundreds and hundreds of people holding up their phones, hoping to capture a photograph of this special, possibly once-in-a-lifetime moment.

BOD accepted the trophy on behalf of the team.

'Congratulations,' said the President. 'You did us all proud!'

You could sense the excitement in the crowd as BOD got ready to lift it. Just before he did, he performed a countdown:

'Three . . . two . . . one . . .'

Then he held the trophy up in the air. And the whole stadium went MAD! Totally and utterly MAD!

And I wondered would I ever again feel as happy as I did in that moment?

We were all exhausted from the effort, but somehow we found the energy to perform a lap of honour.

It was great to get my hands on the trophy even for a few seconds before someone else demanded it. After that, I just wanted to see my family. I walked around the pitch, trying to pick them out of all the thousands of happy faces in the crowd.

Finally, I spotted them, twenty rows back, waving wildly at me and wiping away tears. It was Mum and Dad. And Ian, Shona and Megan. They didn't say anything. And I wouldn't have heard them if they had, of course. But sometimes you can say everything you want with just a look.

None of the players wanted to leave the field – because once we did, the moment would be over. And we knew we might never be all together like this again.

But eventually it was time to go. As I walked back to the dressing room, I saw a group of pitch invaders running towards me. At the front was Conor, followed by Peter, followed by – unless my eyes were deceiving me – four Gardaí in uniform.

'We're friends of Gordon D'Arcy's!' Peter was shouting over his shoulder at them. 'I've known him since I was five years old!'

His glasses fell off onto the ground but he kept on running towards me. Conor reached me first. He jumped up into my arms. I'm sure it looked comical.

'YOU DID IT, DARCE!' he shouted at me. 'YOU DID IT!'

Peter threw his arms around me. I was still holding Conor.

'I'm placing you boys under arrest,' said a big, burly Garda, laying a hand on each of their shoulders.

'Please don't,' I begged them. 'They really *are* my friends! It'd ruin the day for me if you threw them in a cell!'

The Garda nodded sympathetically. 'Maybe this time I'll let them off with a warning,' he said. 'Seeing as you won the match for Ireland today.'

'Em, could I ask you for a favour?' I said.

'What kind of favour?' he asked.

'I was wondering could I get a Garda escort?'

'Where to?'

'Just wait here a minute, will you?'

I went looking for Warren Gatland. He was finishing a TV interview on the pitch.

'Warren,' I said, 'do you mind if I come to the after-match banquet a little bit late?'

'No.' he said. 'Is everything okay?'

'Yeah,' I said. 'I just have to keep a promise to someone.'

# 44 *Just in Time*

I walked back over to where Conor and Peter and the four Gardaí were standing.

'What's going on?' Peter said.

I looked at the Garda.

'So where is it you want to go?' he asked.

And I said, 'Clongowes Wood College, please.'

'This is a very big favour,' he said. For a moment, I thought he was going to refuse, but then he smiled. 'Come on, so. It must be very important if you're willing to leave your moment of glory.'

We climbed into the back of the Garda car – me, Peter and Conor. I was still wearing my Ireland gear and my rugby boots.

'Wow!' Conor said. 'I've always wanted to sit in a squad car!'

The Garda got into the driver's seat and started the engine.

'Can you switch on the siren?' Conor asked. 'I just think it'd add to the excitement.'

The Garda switched on the siren.

Conor looked at me and smiled. 'How COOL is this?' he asked.

'Very cool!' I said.

And then we were off. Soon, we were tearing down the motorway with the blue siren blazing on our way to the school. In front of us, there were two Gardaí on motorbikes. Behind us, there were two more. It reminded me of being on the Ireland team bus in Paris, but no one was shaking their fists at us and shouting, *Allez les bleus!*

Around us, cars pulled quickly into the inside lane to let us past. Drivers strained to see who was in the back of the squad car, probably wondering why we were in such a hurry.

'Could you drive a little bit faster?' I asked.

'I'm sorry,' replied the Garda, shaking his head. 'I'm already right on the speed limit. Wouldn't look good if I was breaking the traffic laws, now would it?'

'How long is left?' I asked Peter.

He looked at his watch.

'If it started on time,' he said, 'then about five minutes.'

'How far away are we?' I asked the Garda.

'About four and a half minutes,' he said.

Exactly four and a half minutes later, we turned off the road and drove up the long driveway towards the school. Our Garda friend switched off the siren.

From a distance, I could see that the game was still in progress.

'Can you drive on the grass?' I asked.

I just thought it would save time.

'No problem at all,' he said.

He crossed the field and pulled to a halt about twenty yards away from the pitch. We jumped out and ran to the sidelines.

There was a big crowd watching the game. From their excitement, I sensed that the game was in the balance.

'What score is it?' Peter asked a woman who was standing nearby.

'St Theresa's are beating St Bridget's 9–7. We're in injury time.'

'Oh no!' Conor said. 'Poor Aoife!'

The woman turned to Conor.

'Do you actually *know* Aoife Kehoe?' she asked.

'Know her?' he said. 'Of course I know her – she's my cousin.'

'I'm Jill Gillespie,' she said. 'I'm the coach of the Ireland schoolgirls team. She's a great player. She's head and shoulders above everyone else out there.'

The woman noticed me standing there in my full Ireland kit.

'Oh,' she said, 'you're Gordon D'Arcy!'

'I am,' I said.

'Well done today. I was listening to it on the radio on the way here. I heard you played very well.'

'No, it was more of a team effort really. Everyone played a part.'

Then we heard a whistle blow.

'The referee's given a penalty!' Conor shouted. 'St Bridget's have a penalty!'

'If Aoife puts this over,' Peter said, 'they'll have won. I don't envy her the pressure, though!'

The problem was that the angle was really difficult.

There was absolute silence as Aoife got down on one knee to place the ball in the tee. Then she stood up and took a long, hard look at the posts.

She measured four steps backwards, then took three more to the side . . .

She looked up at the posts . . .

Then back at the ball . . .

Then up at the posts . . .

Then back at the ball . . .

Then she took a deep breath and ran at the ball. She kicked it and sent it sailing high into the air . . .

. . . and right between the St Theresa's posts!

The referee blew the whistle and Aoife was mobbed by her teammates. In all honesty, I was more pleased for her success than for my own.

She spotted us and gave us a wave. Then her teammates lifted her up on their shoulders and tried to carry her around the pitch. But Aoife insisted they put her down because she wanted to shake hands with the St Theresa's players.

That was a really classy touch.

'I'm just going to go and talk to your cousin,' Jill told Conor. 'She's got a big future ahead of her.'

'Right,' I said, 'I better get to the banquet.'

I noticed that the Garda who drove us here was waiting. I think he kind of enjoyed the excitement of the day, too.

Peter and Conor just nodded.

'Alright,' Conor said, 'well done again, Darce.'

'We'll see you in school on Monday morning,' Peter said.

Then they went to walk away.

'Where do you think you two are going?' I asked.

They turned back to me.

'Back to the dorm,' Peter said. 'I'm going to spend the night studying.'

'No, you're not,' I told him. 'Because you're both coming with me. I'm going to ask Warren if you can come to the banquet.'

Their faces lit up.

'I don't believe it!' Conor said.

'Are you serious?' Peter asked.

'Yes,' I said, 'I'm serious. I want my two best friends to share this moment with me. Although no pranks, Conor – I mean it.'

'There won't be!' he assured me. 'I just can't believe I'm about to meet Paul O'Connell. He's my all-time hero – er, after you, Gordon, obviously.'

I laughed. 'You don't have to say that,' I told him.

'Okay,' he said. 'Let's just say you're a very close second.'

'That's good enough for me!' I said.

We climbed into the back of the squad car again. Our Garda friend put on the siren and soon we were back on the road.

'You won the Grand Slam,' Conor said. 'Aoife kicked a winning penalty, and now we get to hang out with the Ireland team! This is the Best! Day! Ever!'

# 45 'There's Someone Here to See You'

I went back to school the following night. There were no crowds of cheering boys this time. No one sang 'Mill 'Em, Darce'. There was no banner with my name on it. There was no fanfare at all.

And that was exactly how I wanted it.

Some of the boys said some kind things to me. They told me they thought I played really well against Wales. Before, I would have stood around, lapping up the praise, but now I just said, 'Thank you,' and smiled politely and moved along.

Mr Murray said that the second time round I'd understand what comes from working hard and not letting success go to your head. He was right.

The attitude of the teachers towards me didn't change at all.

On Monday morning, two days after the Grand Slam decider, Mr Boyce, my History teacher, said: 'Notwithstanding your heroics against Wales at the weekend, Mr D'Arcy – which, I must say, I very much enjoyed – you were due to hand in an essay this morning on the Life and Times of the Prussian Statesman Otto von Bismarck. It was to be at least eight hundred words in length. Do you have such an essay to give to me today?'

'Yes, Sir,' I said. Because I wrote it when I got back to school the previous night. I handed him my copy book.

My essay was exactly eight hundred words in length – no more, no less. Yes, I'd discovered the importance of hard work on the rugby field. But I hadn't *completely* changed!

Over the weeks that followed, everything settled down again. Steven Varsey put on a lot of weight, which was mainly due to his fondness for sausages. He was knocked out in the first round of Junior Wimbledon, at which point Flash Barry dropped him as a client. Instead, Barry started pursuing the latest sports star to have caught his eye – a young rugby-playing sensation whose exploits for St Bridget's had earned her a call-up to the Ireland schoolgirls team.

One day in early April, Aoife was practising her kicking on the Clongowes pitch. She was sending ball after ball between the posts from different angles and distances, while me, Conor and Peter were running around like Uncle Tim and Auntie Kathleen's chickens, picking up the balls and bringing them back to her. She was in the Ireland squad to play against France – in Paris, of all places!

'You're going to really love it,' I told her. 'Although I wouldn't recommend the snails.'

Aoife sent yet another ball over the bar and that's when I heard the sound of clapping. I looked across and it was Barry.

'Excellent!' he shouted. 'It's no wonder everyone's talking about you as the next big thing!'

Aoife stopped what she was doing as Barry approached her.

'Barry Considine,' he said, introducing himself. 'Agent to the Stars.'

'I know who you are,' Aoife told him.

'Then you'll know that I've represented several sport stars while they were enjoying their moment in the spotlight, including Gordon there – hi, Gordon! – and Steven Varsey, before he got fat. Here, speaking of which, do you want to punch me in the stomach?'

'Why would I want to do that?' Aoife asked.

'You wouldn't! Because it's rock-hard! You'd break your hand and that would be you out of the match in Paris. And we can't have that, can we? Especially with you on the verge of becoming a MAJOR celebrity figure.'

'Don't listen to him!' I told Aoife.

'It's okay, Gordon, I want to hear what he has to say.'

Barry smiled.

'Aoife, you're very talented,' he said. 'For a girl, anyway. You make me your agent and I will turn you into superstar!'

'Wow!' Aoife said. 'Really?'

'Really!'

'He's a liar,' Conor shouted. 'Aoife, say no.'

'Conor,' she said, 'I want to hear his pitch.'

'The pitch is simple,' Barry said. 'You stick with me and I will help you maximize your earning potential for as long as you're at the top.'

I noticed then that he was holding something in his hands. It turned out to be a box.

'I've got something for you,' he said. 'Let's call it a signing-on bonus.'

He lifted the lid and showed her what was inside the box. It was a pair of gold rugby boots. Across the heel of one boot was the word 'TOTAL'. Across the heel of the other was the word 'LEGEND'.

'Wow!' Aoife said. 'They really are something!'

'You want to stand out from the crowd,' Barry told her. 'The most important thing in life is to be noticed.'

Aoife smiled at him.

'You know,' she said, 'I am going to take you up on your offer.'

'To be your agent?' he asked, delighted.

'No,' she said, 'to punch you in the stomach.'

And she did! Right there and then! And she didn't hurt her hand at all! Barry's stomach was as soft as jelly!

He walked off, doubled over, telling Aoife that she would regret that because he could have made her huge – even bigger than Beyoncé.

We all laughed. No one could say that Barry didn't have it coming.

That was when one of the Sixth Year prefects appeared. He shouted at me from the sideline of the pitch.

'Gordon,' he said, 'Mr Cuffe wants to see you in his office. Immediately.'

I was thinking, What could this be about? I haven't played any pranks. I've been attentive in class – sort of. I've handed in all my essays – and every one of them met the minimum word count.

'Sounds like you're in trouble,' Conor said.

I walked to Mr Cuffe's office and knocked twice on the door. He opened it.

'Ah, Mr D'Arcy!' he said.

There was that word again. *Mr.*

'I don't know what I'm being accused of,' I said, 'but I can tell you that it definitely wasn't me.'

He laughed. 'No,' he said, opening the door wider, 'you're not in any kind of trouble – this time anyway. There's someone here to see you.'

'Who is it?' I asked, stepping into the office.

I looked around. And for the second time in a few short months, I was forced to do a double-take. Because sitting in the office was another man I had only ever seen on TV before.

He stood up and extended his hand to me.

'Gordon?' he said. 'I'm Joe Schmidt. Leinster coach.'

'Yes, I know!' I said.

'How are you going?' he asked.

He spoke with an accent that was kind of similar to Warren Gatland's.

'I'm . . . I'm . . . fine,' I said, a little bit lost for words.

'I saw you play,' he said, 'against Wales. You really impressed me.'

'Really?'

And then he said: 'How would you like to come and play for Leinster?'

# GORDON D'ARCY

Gordon D'Arcy was first called up to play for Ireland while he was still at school. He won his first cap in 1999 and his final cap in 2015, making him Ireland's longest-serving international player. Shortly after making his first appearance for his country, he fell out of favour with management because of his 'attitude problems'. But he returned three years later, a better and more mature player. In 2004, he was named the Six Nations Player of the Tournament. He played a total of eighty-two times for his country, scoring seven tries. Partnering Brian O'Driscoll in the centre, he was a vital part of two Six Nations Championship-winning teams, including the Grand Slam team of 2009, and starred in four World Cups. He was also a member of two British and Irish Lions squads. With Leinster, he won three European Cups, a Challenge Cup and four league titles.

You made it to the end of my book – well done! I hope you enjoyed it! I wanted to tell my rugby story in the hope that it would inspire young players to take up the game, to enjoy the game and to stay in the game. Rugby is a fantastic team sport, and it changed my life. I know not everyone gets to wear the Ireland jersey or play for their province – I was one of the lucky ones! – but you can enjoy your rugby at any level. It's all about the teamwork, the skills and the satisfaction you get from putting in a good day's work on the field. Like young Gordon in the story, you can learn as much about yourself as about sport when you're out there playing and challenging yourself to get better.

I get asked lots of questions about my rugby career and the game. I'm always interested to hear what young players think about playing and watching rugby, and the mad questions they can come up with! So here is a selection of questions I'm often asked, answered as best I can.

## Q. What is a typical day in the life of a professional rugby player?

**A.** The great thing about being a rugby player is that every day is different. It depends on the time of the year, what matches are coming up, where you are placed in the team (have you lost your place, or have you taken somebody else's place?) and whether you are match fit or injured. There are different priorities depending on where it is in the season, as well. When the season has started, there's a huge emphasis on being in the gym and working on your fitness. At other times it will be about training moves on the pitch, plus rest, to ensure you peak for big games. Ice baths happen all year round, unfortunately, and eating takes up a lot of time! There's breakfast, pre-training snack, then post-training snack, lunch, post-training snack again, dinner and then a snack before bed. Rugby players have to love their food!

**Q. Who was your role model when you were a kid? Who did you want to be like?**

**A.** I was trying to be like Keith Wood, the hooker who threw the ball into the lineout and then ran hard or kicked the ball. He was everywhere on the field. I then met coach Vinnie Murray and he used to say that it's easy to run around people and much harder to trick them with the ball – by passing and kicking.

**Q. What was the best try you ever scored?**

**A.** I scored a try against France in the Six Nations Championship in 2009. I had been out for a year after breaking my arm in eight places (more on that below!). I had three operations on my arm and almost never played again. During the game against France, I came off the bench in the 63rd minute and managed to wriggle out of some tackles to score a try right next to the post. It helped the team win the match (Ireland 30 – France 21) and it was the first victory in what turned out to be a Grand Slam season for us. It also made me feel that I was properly back playing rugby again, which was a great feeling!

**Q. I mess up sometimes and it makes me want to give up rugby. I feel I'm not as good as the others on my team. How did you cope with the huge ups and downs you went through as a player?**

**A.** Every time I made a mistake, I used to feel that I was letting the team down and then I would get very upset. I talked to my dad about it and he helped me to understand that if you are doing your best and you make a mistake, then it's okay. Mistakes are how you learn to get better, and everyone makes them. The trick is to learn quickly so you don't make the same mistake again – that should be your promise to yourself.

**Q. Who was your most difficult opponent? What was it that made him difficult?**

**A.** My brother Ian was the hardest tackler I ever met and I never managed to score a try against him. Outside my family, I think it was probably Ma'a Nonu of New Zealand. He was my opposite number when I played at outside-centre (usually Brian O'Driscoll's position) for Ireland against the All Blacks in Dublin in 2005. We lost 45–7. Ma'a was the perfect centre: big and physical, really fast, great passer of the ball, plus he knew when to kick – and he had cool dreadlocks, too!

**Q. How do you get over the fear of tackling? How did you tackle players who were bigger than you, like Bastareaud?**

**A.** I did lots and *lots* of tackling practice. I would get Mike Ross to run at me, so I could tackle him when he was going full pelt. I would remember all the training I had done and what the coaches had taught me: keep my balance, keep my feet alive, strong step into contact (low around the legs), wrap my arms around him and take a second step into the tackle. Once I practised it over and over, I was never scared of tackling anyone – no matter what size they were. When you have the technique right, you could take down Tadhg Furlong!

## Q. How did you cope with nerves before you played matches for Ireland?

A. In the early days, I used to get really nervous and afraid of making mistakes. But that was entirely natural. When I played for Ireland and Leinster, quite a lot of people were watching. Literally millions, in fact! I learned to handle it when I realized that nervousness is basically excitement plus fear. The excitement bit is fine. It's the fear that you have to learn to handle. And you can do that by making sure you are properly prepared. It's like an actor stepping out onto the stage. If he's learned his lines inside-out and back-to-front, there's far less of a chance of him messing up in front of the audience. He knows his part. He's in control. And it's the same in rugby. It took a long time for the penny to drop for me. But I discovered that if I practised and trained really well during the week, it made me less nervous and less likely to make mistakes. Once I had practised all the things I needed to do during the match, I started to get really excited about playing and seeing how good I could be.

## Q. How much did losing hurt? And how long did it take you to get over a defeat?

**A.** At the start, I used to think about losing for days and days afterwards, trying to think how I could change it and make it different. My dad said to me, 'Can you change the past?' I said, 'No.' Then he said, 'Will you or your teammates make that mistake again?' I said, 'No.' Then my dad explained that losing can be a good thing if you learn from it and it helps you to get better as a team or as an individual. So I always tried to find a lesson or a positive from every match – even the ones we lost. That way, it didn't prey on my mind and attack my self-confidence, which is very important when you have to get back out there the following week and give your best.

**Q. Name one move by one of your Ireland team-mates that made you think, 'Oh my God, I wish it was me who did that'?**

**A.** When Ronan O'Gara used to kick the ball with a perfect spiral over the head of a winger, in between him and the full-back, and then it would roll perfectly into touch five metres from the corner flag, I used to smile and thank my stars he was on my team! Or every time Rob Kearney jumped up through ten competing players to catch a huge bomb in the air. Catching them was not my speciality!

**Q. What was your worst injury?**

**A.** I once broke my arm in eight places and my wrist in two places – all because I failed to tackle properly. I tried to tackle an Italian opponent and I swung my arm instead of tackling with my shoulder. My forearm hit the point of his elbow and the bones just exploded. It took three operations to put it back together again. I always tackled with my shoulder, nice and low, after that.

**Q. Are ice baths as awful as they sound?**

**A.** They are worse! They are so, so cold! The longer you stay in them, the better they are for you. The drawback is that when you stay in there for ages, your legs stop working, so when you get out it is nearly impossible to walk to the shower to warm up again!

**Q. Did you ever make a really embarrassing mistake on the pitch?**

**A.** I'm going to tell you about something that happened to me once but I've always been too embarrassed to talk about – until now. One time, when I was playing a schools match for Clongowes, I picked the ball out of a ruck and dived over the line with it. I grounded the ball, then started jumping up and down in celebration. But my teammates didn't celebrate with me. They were looking at me very strangely indeed. And that's when I realized my mistake. It wasn't the tryline at all. It was the 22. I ran back to the full-back position with my face as red as a tomato!

**Q. Any other embarrassing incidents?**

**A.** Again, I don't know why I'm revealing this, but here goes. I used to pack my bag the night before every game. Then, I always checked it before I got on the team bus to make sure everything I needed was in there. But once I forgot to check, and off I went on the bus to the Aviva. When I reached the dressing room, I discovered that I'd forgotten my boots! I had to borrow a pair from the physio. They were bright yellow and not a good fit. Needless to say, I didn't have a good game that day.

**Q. Any more you'd like to get off your chest?**

**A.** Another time, when I was playing for Ireland, I was coming out onto the pitch after half-time. I was late and I was changing into a fresh jersey as I was running. Because the jersey was over my head, I didn't see a man standing in front of me. Bang! I ran straight into him. It must have looked funny to everyone else, but I don't think he was laughing!

**Q.** **Did anyone ever pull down your shorts, like Conor did to young Gordon?**

**A.** As a practical joke by teammates, it happened more times than I can remember. But it also happened to me once in the course of a big match – accidentally, of course. I was playing for Leinster against Leicester Tigers. I had the ball. Manu Tuilagi tried to tackle me around the waist and he grabbed a hold of my shorts. I continued running and dragged him along for about ten metres. And then I became aware that my shorts were falling down. With every step I took, they got lower and lower and lower! All I could think was, Everyone in the stadium and everyone watching at home can see my underpants!

**Q.** **Who was the fastest you played with and against?**

**A.** The fastest player I ever played with was my Leinster and Ireland teammate Denis Hickie. He played on the wing and was an absolute flier. It came as no surprise to me when I found out that he had represented Ireland in the 100m at schools level and had a personal best time of 10.8 seconds, which is very fast indeed! (Usain Bolt can do it in 9.58!) Some people say he might have represented Ireland at the Olympics if he had chosen athletics over rugby. The fastest player I ever played against was the South African winger Bryan Habana. When he took off, there was no catching him. In fact, he once raced a cheetah – how cool is that?!!!

**Q. Did you ever think you might be too small to play rugby?**

**A.** I'm 5'10", which is relatively short for a modern-day rugby player. I was never the biggest or the fastest player in any of the teams I played in. Instead, I made sure that I was very hard to tackle with the ball. I developed dancing feet and I always tried to attack space rather than contact. When I was tackling, having fast feet and being so low to the ground meant that I could chop tackle (around their ankles) and my team-mates would spot the offload if it came. Small can be good. You just have to make sure you know how to turn it into an advantage.

**Q. Did you ever do a big, flashy celebration after scoring a try?**

**A.** I used to do them, but then I hurt myself doing a swan dive. I landed on my knee and had to go off injured. I decided to keep my celebrations simple after that!

**Q. What one tip would you give a young player hoping to make it in rugby?**

**A.** The easiest skill to master in rugby is the ability to beat defenders by running with the ball. It is much harder to pass the ball. Know why you're passing and when to do it. The best players in the world always do the most damage when they're passing the ball rather than running with it.

**If you'd like to put a question to Gordon, go to gordonsgamebook@gmail.com. You never know, your question might end up featuring in Book 2 of *Gordon's Game*! And huge thanks to Erris McCarthy of Boyne RFC (u12) for helping to compile the questions here.**

# ACKNOWLEDGEMENTS

*Gordon D'Arcy's acknowledgements:*

I had the pleasure of playing rugby for over 25 years, enjoying some incredible experiences and making fantastic friends along the way. I genuinely never thought I would write a book, and had it not been for a passing conversation with my sister, this book might never have seen the light of day. It has been such an enjoyable time reminiscing, smiling and sometimes cringing trying to remember everything for this book. The end result has exceeded my wildest dreams, and I want to thank everyone involved.

Thank you to Paul Howard and Faith O'Grady for helping me to bring this to life. To Patricia Deevy and everyone at Penguin Ireland, thank you for staying the course with me, and to Rachel Pierce for pulling this all together. Thanks to Alan Nolan for capturing the essence of the book with your superb artwork.

Thank you to Mum and Dad, my big brother Ian and sisters Shona and Megan. We had fun making these memories and it was lovely to think back over all those years.

For Lennon and Soleil, I hope this makes you smile, and remember that every word is true!

Most importantly, my beautiful wife Aoife, thank you for your unwavering support in everything I do.

*Paul Howard's acknowledgements:*

Enormous thanks to Gordon D'Arcy for daring to tell the story of his Ireland career (sort of) in such a fun and imaginative way. Thank you for inviting me to collaborate with you in bringing it to young readers and for all the hard work you did in making it happen. A massive thank you to Rachel Pierce, not only for a great editing job but for all the expert guidance you brought to the task of turning this into a book for children. Grateful thanks to Phil Twomey and Lorraine Levis of Penguin Random House, Elaina Ryan of Children's Books Ireland and Erris McCarthy of Boyne RFC (u12), who read the first draft and offered invaluable advice. And thank you to Patricia Deevy and Michael McLoughlin for all the patience and guidance you offered when the idea was still forming in our heads. Thanks to my agent, Faith O'Grady, for getting behind the idea right from the beginning. Thanks to artist Alan Nolan for your wonderful illustrations. Thanks to Cliona Lewis, Patricia McVeigh, Brian Walker, Aimée Johnson, Carrie Anderson, Orla King and everyone at Penguin Ireland for your professionalism and endless positivity. And a special word of thanks, as always, to Mary, my very wonderful wife.

*Celebrating 25 years of changing the lives of children
and families affected by serious illness*

www.barretstown.org